DEATH
BELOW
DECK

DEATH BELOW DECK

Douglas Kiker

 RANDOM HOUSE NEW YORK

Library of Congress Cataloging-in-Publication Data
Kiker, Douglas.
Death below deck / by Douglas Kiker.
p. cm.
ISBN 0-679-40022-2
I. Title.
PS3561.I366D44 1991
813'.54—dc20 90-42612

Manufactured in the United States of America
24689753   23456789   98765432
First Edition

*To all my friends at NBC News
from the Good Old Days. Hell of
a lot of fun, wasn't it?*

DEATH BELOW DECK

1

A FEW DEEP BREATHS of tangy salt air is supposed to work wonders on a person with a hangover, but it didn't do much for me that morning. I was weak, I was woozy, and I had a world-class headache.

I parked my old Ford station wagon in the driveway that circled in front of the big yellow house on Clam Pond. A black maid in uniform answered the bell and led me through the center hall, out to the back porch, where I stood uneasily for a moment, gazing across the lawn at a huge yawl that was tied up at the water's edge of the pond.

"Either that boat is cockeyed or I am," I said by way of greeting to Bitsy Binford after the maid announced me.

She was sitting in a wicker chair, reading a morning copy of the *Cape Cod Times*. She placed the newspaper aside and, peering over the top of her half-frame reading glasses, inspected me, then the yawl, at some length. "Maybe a little of both," she said at last. "It seems the boat's aground, and you look about ten degrees off center yourself, McFarland. Now come over here and give an old buddy a kiss." Then she smiled.

Here was a comfortable corner at the left end of the long porch, a proper porch with a wooden floor painted slate gray and with a baby-blue ceiling. A square tan sisal mat defined the area, its four corners weighed down by healthy ferns contained in large clay pots. Thin cane blinds, lowered halfway to the porch's banister railing, shaded the spot from the early morning sun. Overhead a wooden ceiling fan paddled around at quarter-speed. The cushions of a green metal platform glider and two white wicker chairs were covered with a bright green chintz print. Copies of the early Monday morning editions of *The Boston Globe* and *The New York Times* lay at her feet. A white wicker coffee table with a glass top held a stack of other newspapers still encased in their mailing wrappers, a black cellular telephone, and a silver tray that held the morning mail.

Bitsy Binford rose from the chair she sat in, and I walked over and kissed her on both cheeks as she offered them, one after another. The same perfume. I never knew its name, but I still remembered the scent. I got to know it well during the two years I had occupied the desk directly behind hers in the city room of my old Chicago newspaper, back in the days when new cars had tail fins and men wore hats.

Bitsy squeezed my hands firmly and looked me over, closely and at considerable length. "You could use a shave, and you smell like Hooligan's bar. But not too bad. In fact, you've improved with age, McFarland."

"Then that makes two of us, Bitsy."

4

She waved my gallantry away impatiently, having none of it. "Don't hand me that, Mac. I've got a mirror in my bathroom."

She had not aged well. Her face was wrinkled and creased with countless lines that had ploughed through her skin since I had last seen her, and her hair, black as a crow's wing during our newspaper days, was silver-white and closely cropped. It was the face of a woman who looked much older than I knew her to be, sixty-four, thirteen years older than I was. Once slender, willowy, now she was skinny. The white slacks she wore were a full size too large for her, and her navy-blue cotton pullover sweater looked as though it had been borrowed from a big brother. Over the years Bitsy had shrunk a lot.

"No doubt it's my eyes. I know I need new glasses," I said. "But I'd swear you look about the same."

"Ever the gentleman. You always were. Sit down, Mac. In the glider. You and I have some catching up to do."

I took a seat. She picked up a small crystal bell from the coffee table, a gentle summons that immediately produced the maid again. The young woman's gray-black uniform dress was covered by a starched white apron. She had slightly slanted brown eyes, and cheekbones any high-fashion model would have envied. Her skin was more sand tan than it was black.

"Miss Bitsy?" she whispered.

"Coffee, Mac?"

"A couple of gallons."

"Miss Bitsy, Lily Dell's done baked some of her pecan rolls this morning, if the gentleman would care for one," the maid said.

"I'm sure he would, Wyvonny."

"I'm gone bring you one, too."

"No, no. I couldn't eat a bite."

"Living on black coffee, Miss Bitsy."

"You scoot, Wyvonny."

"Yes'um." The maid hurried away. Did she curtsy, ever so slightly, to Bitsy before she left?

"Lily Dell's pecan rolls melt in your very mouth," Bitsy said. "We bring the pecans up from home. You can't beg, borrow, or steal an unshelled pecan on Cape Cod, you know."

"I've heard that. In cocktail-party talk."

She laughed, a throaty laughter that had not changed. "That wit's still there, I see."

"What else comes up on the underground railroad?"

"A few hams."

"Sure goes good with grits, I'm told."

"Well, they do taste better than those packinghouse things they pump full of water. That's all there is to it. Peanut-fed hogs, and the hams are cured in our own smokehouse."

"What do you do about drinking water? Bottle it from the creek back down home?"

"Well, some things haven't changed. You're still on me about my Southern ways, I see."

"You were the first Southern belle I ever knew, Bitsy. And that accent's still as strong as ever."

Bitsy was born and raised in the South, the daughter of a university professor of economics. After graduation from the University of Georgia, she had worked for newspapers in Brunswick, Georgia, and in Atlanta before com-

6

ing to Chicago. When I became a staff reporter there she was covering city hall, the toughest beat in town.

"Still making fun of the way I talk, I see," she said.

"Well, I'll say it again. Accent and hot temper and all, you were one of the best newspaper reporters I ever knew."

"The steel magnolia. Bitsy the bitch. That's what they called me behind my back."

I looked into her eyes. "I had a crush on you back then. You knew that."

Her sudden blush told me that, yes, she had known it, and it pleased her to recall those days when she had been Bitsy Zimmerman, big byliner and beautiful bitch goddess. "You were a baby when you came to the paper," she said.

"I was a Korean War veteran, a combat marine. I didn't think of myself as a baby."

"I had just broken up with a man when you were hired. You never knew about that."

"Are you kidding? Some asshole lawyer who kept sending you flowers? It was the talk of the city room. I knew all about it. As I recall, he was married."

"Every girl has to have one, it seems. But you and I did have one night together. Remember?"

"Of course."

"Liar. Where? When?"

"Down in Springfield. At that little mom-and-pop motel."

"You do remember. I'm thrilled."

"It was the only place we could find, because the legislature was in session." She and I had been doing a story

7

together about a state senator from Chicago who was accepting bribes from a dozen different contractors. We sent him to jail. My first big story.

"You told me that night you loved me. Do you remember *that*?" she asked. "A young man's declaration of love always means a lot to an older woman, McFarland."

"But you never let it go any further than that one night. Do *you* remember *that*? You kept putting me off. Until I finally gave up and found somebody else."

"Paula. She was a secretary to one of the municipal-court judges. And more of your own tender age. I knew about Paula."

"Paula lived on french fries and chocolate milk. That's all she really liked to eat." I smiled. "I had forgotten about her."

"Just another screw. Like me. I never."

"Come on, Bitsy."

"Oh, I like to think of myself that way. An old woman's daydreams. A damn good piece of ass. Wasn't I?"

"I thought I'd died and gone to heaven and was screwing an angel."

"Well, you knocked this particular angel up. I had to get an abortion."

"Christ, Bitsy. I never knew."

"It was my decision. You were too young for me, McFarland."

Our eyes held for a long moment, this old woman's and mine. It was as if it all had happened during a different lifetime. I didn't know what to say. I wondered if I had been in her thoughts all these years. She certainly hadn't been in mine.

"How long did you stay at the paper after I left?" she asked. "I know you won a Pulitzer."

"Twenty-five years. I stayed there for twenty-five years. A long time." I didn't tell Bitsy I had been fired abruptly when the paper's ownership changed hands a year ago and a gang of Neanderthals took over. I tried to encourage people to believe I left on my own, out of principle, honor, pride. Shit like that.

"Did you ever get married, Mac? I often wondered about that."

"And divorced." After I discovered that my wife was screwing the dentist she worked for. I didn't tell Bitsy that, either, nor that I still was not quite divorced, only legally separated, because the woman was playing some kind of game with me.

"I guess everybody breaks up these days," she said. "Although I'm sure the woman must have been quite insane to let you get away."

"Her name's Earline. If that gives you the slightest hint."

She laughed. "I'm trying to imagine the body she must have. Well, I never."

"How'd you find out I'm living up here on the Cape?" When Earline became the subject of conversation, I always wanted to change it.

"Your article in the Sunday *Globe* on whale-watching. It said at the bottom you were living here in North Walpole."

"I free-lance for them."

"Well, you write good news copy as well as ever. I called Boston and got your phone number here in North Walpole."

"And a woman answered and said I don't live there anymore."

"She was nice enough about it. She gave me the number at the Buckaneer Inn, where I found you." She hesitated. "That wasn't Earline, was it?"

"God, no. Earline's back in Chicago. It was just a friend. I'd rather not go into the details."

"There I go, still trying to treat you like a kid brother."

Wyvonny reappeared and served us coffee from a silver pot. The cups and saucers were as thin and weightless as tissue. The pecan rolls, served with sweet, saltless country butter, were hot from the oven, and the coffee was lightly laced with chicory. On a shady corner of the porch a caged Gloucester canary sang.

I bit into my pecan roll. "As God is my witness, I shall never go hungry again. Isn't that what Scarlett O'Hara said? When she was digging taters? In fact, this place looks a little like Tara. Why an Old South antebellum mansion in New England?"

"My late husband's great-grandfather built it. It's almost an exact duplicate of our place back home. What do you think?"

"It's a magnificent place. I've wondered who lived here, so much land around it, so many pine trees, that high privet hedge, and it sits so far in from the road and so far back from the shore of the pond. I thought maybe Greta Garbo, somebody like that."

"I know it looks out of place up here. Great-grandfather Binford was a Princeton man. In his day, well-born Southern boys went to Princeton, if they went north to college at all. The family story is that one of his roommates was from North Walpole, and he visited here and liked it. The Binford family has been summering here for generations."

"Including you?"

"Oh, goodness yes. For years and years. This really is a second home to the children. Not that they're children anymore."

"I just got here last winter. I had no idea you were an old North Walpolian. I lost track of you after you got married. I never did meet your husband."

"I barely did. Freeport died of a heart attack six months after we were married."

"Bitsy, I didn't know that. I'm sorry."

"Ah, it all happened so long ago and so quickly that I barely remember him, tell you the truth. I kept the poor man's picture in my bedroom for some years, then one day I looked at it and thought to myself, You don't really know this man. I put it away. I know that sounds horrible."

"I remember it was a real whirlwind romance. Everybody in the city room was taken by surprise. Including me."

"We met at a party during the 1956 Democratic National Convention."

"Which was held in Chicago. They nominated Stevenson again."

"I was covering the Chicago delegates. Freeport was there, writing for his paper back home. A lark really. A widower with three kids. We sort of fell together."

"I'm confused. I thought Freeport is the name of the town in Georgia where you live."

"It is. Freeport was named for the town. When he was

1 1

born, his mother wanted to name him Jessup, her maiden name. For weeks and weeks it was Jessie this and little Jessie that. His father didn't say a word. Then, at the christening, when the priest asked, What shall this child be called?, out of the blue his father said *Freeport*! Which makes sense, since the man who built this house also built and named the town."

"Freeport had no other family to lend you a hand after he died?"

"No. He had an older brother killed on Iwo Jima, a sister who died of cancer."

"So you were left with three stepchildren to raise."

"And a big farm to manage. *And* the *Freeport Coastal Advocate* to publish. It was not exactly what I had in mind for the future when I was covering city hall in Chicago, I can tell you that."

I glanced around. "You seem to have done okay."

"I worked my butt off for years, Mac. But it seems I got a head for business from my father. And newspapering I knew. Also, I had good people around me. Freeport Communications is in good shape."

"Are you still running things?"

"Heavens no. A manager looks after the farm, has for years. And my youngest stepdaughter's husband took over as president of the company three years ago. I moved up to board chairman. That's his boat down there."

"Will you be angry if I tell you I never heard of Freeport Communications?"

She laughed. "No reason why you should. Everything we do is small. Small dailies. Small weeklies. Small radio and television stations. Some small cable companies. No major markets."

"It sounds like you've done all right."

"A few years back, if you were a publisher in a small town close to a big, growing city, the opportunity was obvious. Commuters from the city move in. The little town keeps growing. Local merchants have no other place to advertise."

"And there you were, ready to take their money."

"It didn't take a genius. The *Coastal Advocate* and our little radio station kept making more and more money and becoming more valuable, and I used them as collateral to buy others like them. And I did it before the big boys caught on."

"You own a lot of them?"

She smiled. "Quite a few."

"All over the country?"

"No, but all over the South."

"Bitsy, you've become a media queen."

"A corn-pone, two-bit Kay Graham is more like it."

"You never got remarried? You would have been a sexy, young gay widow."

"Twice. Neither was very successful, I'm sorry to say."

I didn't say anything. I was sorry I had asked. How's your father these days? He's still dead.

"First time, the county attorney. A divorcé. And a handsome man. I had the idea he'd make a marvelous company president. Except he tried to beat me up. Can you imagine that? I threw him out, out of the house, out of the county, and out of the goddam state before I was through."

"He's probably in the South Seas somewhere today," I said. "Dirty, gaunt, on whiskey, a shadow of his former self."

"I don't know where he is and don't care."

"I can't imagine a man raising his hand to you, Bitsy. You were a tough cookie."

"It was like leaving on a sailing trip on a small boat with people you think are close friends. A day out of port you realize you've made a horrible mistake."

"You said there were two."

"The second was another widower. With five grown daughters, all of them perfect bitches. I never had a chance. I just up and left after a year or so. I don't even count that one."

An old black man had appeared from around one corner of the house, walking backward as he carefully uncoiled a garden hose.

"You, Lincoln, now don't you forget to mix some rusty nails in the dirt before you put in those new hydrangeas I bought," Bitsy called to him.

He grinned and held up an old coffee can. "Full of 'em. I stop and pick up every nail I come across for a solid week now, Miss Bitsy."

"Thank you, Lincoln."

"Lincoln," I said. "Why, he must be named after that president who freed the slaves."

"Lily Dell's husband. They've both been with the family for years and years, since before I arrived. That Lincoln can make a walking stick sprout."

"Why rusty nails?"

"Now surely an old Cape Codder like you knows that

trick. The oxide in the rusty iron makes the flowers h~~
Otherwise, they're that washed-out pink."

"I'll add that to my growing storehouse of Down Eas~~
knowledge," I said.

I tried to lift the cup and saucer from the arm of the glider, but I didn't have sufficient strength in the fingers of my right hand. I lost control of both of them and spilled the coffee in my lap. Even a minor stroke can leave a person that way. It was not something I liked to talk about.

"Well! You are hung over, aren't you?" Bitsy cried.

"Sorry. It's really not a hangover. I had . . . Yes, I guess I am." Why go into that? It was one more thing that suddenly had gone wrong with the new life I had tried to put together for myself in North Walpole, on olde Cape Cod.

Wyvonny, who had been standing silently inside the screened door waiting for a summons, rushed out without a word and took the dishes away quickly, after using my napkin to mop up the coffee spill.

Bitsy waved at me in dismissal, an old, familiar gesture of hers I remembered from our newspaper days. "No harm done," she said. "More coffee?"

"I don't think I'd better try again right away."

She looked around the yard. "Then let's take a walk around the yard. The sun will dry your trousers for you." We walked off the porch together.

"This is my first summer here," I said.

"I feel as if I've been coming up here forever."

"I got here last winter. The place is transformed now."

August on Cape Cod. The place had become infested with tourists, all of whom seemed to have pockets lined with money, and I mean big bills. There were long waiting es outside the popular restaurants; the college kids who worked as waiters and waitresses in them worked like dogs, then drenched themselves in their parents' pools in the early mornings. No vacancy signs were happily posted at every hotel and motel from Falmouth to Provincetown. Signs of offerings had blossomed, and shops and stores, closed for the long winter, had reopened. The beaches were crowded, the roads were filled with long lines of automobiles, and every harbor and inlet was alive with boats. Suddenly, it seemed, everybody in the world had discovered Cape Cod.

It is an air-conditioned peninsula that juts out like a cocked, beckoning finger off the Massachusetts coast, cooled by winds blowing off the North Atlantic, and people have long found relief there from the heat and congestion of the big Eastern Seaboard cities.

This was my first summer there, and I had discovered that many parts of the place, smaller and quieter spots not yet invaded by day-trippers or ravaged by land developers, were indeed as beautiful and unspoiled as advertisements and travel articles proclaimed them to be. Certainly paradise would have been to have lived there half a century ago.

Its antebellum styling made Belle Haven—its name was on a small sign at the driveway entrance—seem special but not unseemly. The yellow mansion sat within five or six secluded, pine-filled, and expensive acres of land on the western shore of a saltwater inlet off Nantucket Sound named Clam Pond. Across the way, as Bitsy and I strolled that morning, I could see the house where I had been

16

living until things fell apart on me, and I wondered what Kate Bingham was up to at this hour. To hell with that.

Belle Haven, by the look of it, was both a family compound and a southern outpost. There was a fenced cutting-flower garden that, from a distance, looked like an oil hurriedly done as a house present during a summer visit by some minor Impressionist. There was a gray-shingled gardener's shed at the far edge of the back lawn—Lincoln's retreat, I guess. I imagined him sitting inside it on an afternoon, counting rusty nails—and at the water's edge there was an octagon-shaped gazebo, no doubt a fine place to watch sunsets. The entire left side of the lawn was a golf putting course, its holes marked by small, numbered flags, red numbers on a white field, and the right side was spiked with hoops and stakes and limed for croquet. All that was missing was a smokehouse, a family burial plot, and a weeping willow tree.

"What a truly beautiful place," I said.

"It ought to be, what I pay for gardeners. Lincoln just putters. He's too old to keep after a yard this size."

"You seem to have a full house. Lots of cars out front."

"Three servants, Freeport Junior, my stepson, my step-daughter Sally Ann and her husband Peter, my step-daughter Polly and her husband Cyril. And, oh, my editor in chief's up for a visit. Freeport Junior and Polly and Cyril were up before dawn to go out on a whale-watching boat."

"Who's the oldest?"

"Polly's forty-two. And it makes me feel old just to say it. Sally Ann's thirty-five. Why, Freeport Junior's thirty-one now. They do get away from you, like they say." She took my arm, and we strolled down to the cut-flower garden.

"I see now where all the flowers in the house come from."

"We have the fence to keep the rabbits out. This really is Lincoln's territory. It's all he does, to tell you the truth."

"Yoo-hoo. Mother Bitsy?" A young woman had walked out of what appeared to be a new addition to the main house. It was a separate house, really, connected to the Belle Haven mansion by a covered red-brick walkway.

"Sally Ann, my dear. Did you sleep well?" Bitsy asked.

"Yes, thank you. Any mail for us?" She had the look of the classic Cape Cod summer wife, tanned and healthy-looking, her hair lightened by exposure to the sun. She was wearing a denim wraparound skirt, a pink button-down shirt, and sandals. Her hair was tied back with a plaid ribbon.

"No mail, but there's coffee on the porch," Bitsy said.

"Thanks, but I'm on my way to Purl One to pick up some yarn I ordered. Do you need anything from town?"

"I really can't think of a thing. What are you working on now?"

"Still those darn seat covers with that Mondrian design."

"Come and meet an old Chicago friend of mine. Mac McFarland. My daughter Sally Ann."

Sally Ann smiled and waved at me, but didn't move. "How *are* you? So nice to *see* you!" she called out.

"Sally Ann is a crackerjack at needlepoint," Bitsy said. "You should see some of the things she's done. Museum pieces."

"Have you seen Peter?"

"No. Probably at the marina buying boat supplies."

"I was wondering if he needs anything. I swear, since he took possession of that boat, he's been in another world."

"I'm sure he doesn't."

She waved at us. "Bye-bye, then. Give me a call at Purl One if you think of anything." She walked over and got into a Volvo station wagon parked in the driveway and pulled away. Summer wives, I had discovered, always seemed to be on their way somewhere, usually in Volvos; a few of them, perhaps, to illicit holiday affairs, but most of them to the farmers' market.

"That's a handsome new addition," I said to Bitsy.

"Sally Ann and Peter needed it with their two children. Their own place, in effect."

"The builder got a little confused, didn't he? There's no door at the end of the walkway. It leads to a wall."

"You can build an addition without a building permit in North Walpole. Peter's an impatient sort. He didn't want to be bothered with municipal red tape, so he built a house and added the walkway. It doesn't lead to a door because it doesn't have to. It's called a mother-in-law addition here."

The new addition was painted a more vivid yellow than the old house, and its neoclassic design, executed no doubt by some bright, wry architect who had photos to show friends, was in ballpark harmony with that of the mansion, a young, fresh-faced daughter holding—the covered walkway—a graying mother's hand.

"Let's walk down to the dock. I'm sure you'd like to take a closer look at the boat," Bitsy said. She took my arm.

The big yawl had a royal-blue hull with a gold stripe, a teak deck, Hood sails, and a wheel covered with tan glove leather.

"Well, what do you think?" Bitsy asked.

"It still looks cockeyed to me."

"I think it's aground."

"Your son-in-law ought to learn how to sail it. *Comchi*? What's that? Some Indian name?"

Bitsy smiled. "No. It's short for communications chief. Peter's the president of Freeport Communications, remember? Sally Ann's husband."

"It's a little hard to keep this dynasty straight. There's enough electronic gear on that mast to bring in Tokyo Rose on a clear night. I can tell you that."

"Radar, sonar, a cellular phone, television, a computer up-link dish, everything. Peter had it outfitted as a floating office. Fifty-six feet and practically all-electric. You push a button and the mainsail unfurls. Push another one and the anchor comes up. It doesn't sail itself, of course—but it's the next thing to it. The *Comchi* is user-friendly.

"I don't think there's a bigger boat in all of North Walpole. Certainly not one that's aground. Clam Pond's too shallow for a boat this size. He should never have brought it in here."

"That's what the Coast Guard said. He motored it in at high tide yesterday at noon."

"And when the tide went out, the keel sank into the mud."

"This was the first time he'd ever brought it in here. He's just bought it. And he's in love with it, of course.

Freeport Junior helped him sail it up from Bristol, Rhode Island, from the boatyard there, after Peter took delivery."

"They do have charts, with depths recorded."

"Yes, but Peter has always thought that circumstances should fit his actions and not the other way around."

"Well, it's still a good-looking boat. Lead keel, probably no real harm done."

"The Coast Guard's supposed to come and pull it free around noon today. Would you like to go aboard and take a look around? I'm sure Peter wouldn't mind."

"Sure." We walked across the gangplank and stepped aboard the boat, into the cockpit.

Everything was new, right out of the yard with not a scratch, not the first mark of wear and tear on anything. The chrome-plated fittings were spotless, and of the latest and most advanced design. The navy-blue mainsail cover was bright and unfaded, the teakwood deck as yet unbleached by the sea, the glove-leather wheel cover still unsoiled by dirty hands.

"Well, what do you think? Pretty spiffy, huh?" Bitsy asked.

"It looks like it should be in some boat show. It must have cost a bundle."

"Almost a million. Can you believe it?"

"That's a bundle, all right."

"Certainly when you think of what you and I used to make on the paper. I was not especially enthusiastic about the purchase."

Comchi sat motionless in the water, firmly aground, the hull listing at four or five degrees to starboard.

"How do you come to know so much about boats?" Bitsy asked.

"I don't. Just a little. I was a marine, remember? They teach you seamanship in boot camp. Lots of marines serve on-board ships."

"Well, what do you think? No structural damage, you say?"

"No, just stuck. Your son-in-law's bought himself one more beautiful toy. Where is he, anyway? You said at the marina?"

"No, down there, I think. Take a look below. You'll find him."

I climbed down the ladder into the main cabin. Bitsy didn't follow me. She waited up in the cockpit, giving me time to take it all in. Then she called to me, "Well, what do you think?"

I didn't answer her. I couldn't bring myself to answer her right away.

"Mac? What do you think?"

"What do I *think*? What do you think I think? Damn it, Bitsy, you know what I think. I think he's dead is what I think!" I shouted at her.

2

THERE WERE HOLES in both soles of Peter Stallings's Topsiders. There was a ragged hole in the left knee of his white duck trousers, as if he had spent a lot of time in prayer, a hole in one elbow of his yellow cotton Polo sweater, and there was a very large and ragged hole high in the back of his head, what little of the back of his head that was left.

His body lay sprawled on the couch on the port side of the boat's main, spacious cabin, his face to one side, his eyes wide open, as if he had been both surprised and horrified by what he realized was happening to him. *My God, I'm dead,* he looked as if he had thought, a second before he was. His head lay in a thick red-brown blot of dark blood. He had been shot through his open mouth.

His left hand lay across his stomach, and his right arm fell away from his body, the right hand almost touching the deck of the boat's cabin. A gun, a black revolver, lay on the deck an inch or so away from his right hand. Two glasses and a nearly empty bottle of Remy Martin cognac were on the table in front of the couch his body lay on.

God, he was an ugly, vulgar sight. As a marine and as a news reporter who started out on a police beat, I've seen more than my share of violent deaths. People who die that way look as if they had just been initiated into a private club, taken away forever into that exclusive membership, yet still with you, part of you, because they died with their bodies in movement, not in repose. Violent death awes me. Suicide always sickens, the ultimate reproach to loved ones. I hate the sight of them.

Peter Stallings had blond hair and a trim, tanned body—a handsome guy, and far too young to be lying there like that.

I made myself step over and take the man's right wrist in my hand and feel for a pulse, although I knew full well I wouldn't find one. One more blown away *Comchi* he was. And a new complication in my own life I did not need.

"Bitsy!" I shouted. "You get down here!"

"No! I've seen him. I *found* him, for God's sake," she called back immediately.

I climbed up the ladder to the cockpit and took several deep breaths of the sweetest air I had inhaled in a long time.

"You are white as a sheet, Mac," Bitsy said. "Are you going to be sick?"

"Just shut your mouth."

"An old police reporter like you. I'm surprised."

"I said shut up, Bitsy," I said. "What the hell are you trying to do, pulling a trick like this on me?"

"What do you think? He's killed himself, hasn't he? Blown his brains out, from what I could see."

"Why didn't you tell me before I climbed down there?"

She stared out at the waters of Clam Pond as if she were trying to remember something, a forgotten name, an important date, an urgent errand, and she looked as if she would start shivering uncontrollably when she did remember. This was, after all, her son-in-law.

"I don't know. I couldn't bring myself to do it. Say it. I don't know." She was shivering now.

"You say you found him?"

"Yes, a few minutes before I called you at the Buckaneer Inn. I was going to call you later today, but the minute I found Peter, I had to call you. For some reason I got it in my mind, Mac will take care of this. Thank God you could come."

"Why did you come down here earlier this morning?"

"Peter asked me last night to meet him on the porch this morning at eight for a cup of coffee. To talk business. He didn't show up. I rang Sally Ann over at the addition. He wasn't there, either. Sally Ann said he hadn't been there all night. She assumed he'd slept on the boat. It was his new play-pretty, and it was hard to get him off it."

"So you came down here looking for him?"

"I waited a little while longer, had coffee, then walked down here. I called from the dock. No answer, so I came on board, and there he was. The way you saw him."

"Obviously his wife doesn't know anything about it yet, the way she acted. Have you called the police?"

"I wanted a little time to sort this through and figure out what I have to do next."

"What you do next is call the cops. There's a dead man down there. Bitsy, you also covered a police beat in your day."

"Long enough to know an hour or two doesn't make much difference one way or another." She looked at me defiantly.

"Look, the police chief here in North Walpole is a friend of mine. I'll call him for you."

"Chief Simmons?"

"Yes. Listen, when you found your son-in-law like that, did you touch anything? Turn his body over? Shake him, feel his pulse? Anything?"

"God, no. He was so obviously dead, and I was scared out of my wits. I turned and went up that ladder as fast as I could."

"Let's go back to the house, and I'll call the cops."

"There's a cellular phone right here in the cockpit. In that box. Peter always had to have instant communication right at his fingertips."

The dispatcher at North Walpole Police Headquarters told me that Noah Simmons was cruising the town but checked in on his car radio every few minutes.

Noah ran a tight ship, especially during the busy summer months of July and August when so many temporary "specials" were added to the force to deal with the larger crowds. Most of them were off-duty security guards from Hyannis who didn't know the territory all that well. Noah was obliged to add them to his small permanent force because the town's population swelled from a winter low of around five thousand to thirty thousand, more on the weekends, and kids, always quick to detect the absence of authority, tried to get away with all sorts of mischief. Noah hated these two months.

"Is there a message? Where can he reach you?" the dispatcher asked.

"Tell Noah to get over to Belle Haven on Clam Pond as quickly as possible. Somebody's dead. Tell him McFarland called." I hung up.

"Is there anything else we should do before the police arrive?" Bitsy asked.

"Not that I can think of," I said.

"Then let's get off this boat," she said. "It gives me the creeps."

We crossed the gangway to the wooden dock and walked together across the lawn, back toward the house. The mid-August morning had a deep, fresh feeling about it that promised a sunny but hazy high-season Cape Cod day.

"Bitsy, did that guy have a drinking problem? There was a brandy bottle in the cabin that was nearly empty."

She hesitated. "Peter . . . was having all sorts of problems. And most of them are my problems now."

Neither of us spoke again. We strolled at Bitsy's leisurely pace, as if we were out inspecting the new hydrangeas, as if we were thirty years younger. She didn't offer any unsolicited information, and I didn't ask any further questions. I think we both knew that once we got back on that porch, Peter Stallings's death would become the overriding reality for her. And I still had a headache.

There was a man standing on the porch, watching us

as we walked across the lawn. He had a glass in his hand. "Ho ho ho," he called out.

Bitsy shielded her eyes with the palm of her hand and looked at him.

"Ho ho ho," the man said again. He wasn't laughing.

"Oh God," she said. "This is more than I can handle."

The man looked to be in his late fifties and counting—a few years younger than Bitsy, but only a few. He was plain ugly, from top to bottom, with wild and unruly hair that fought a comb, a pockmarked complexion, and a face like a mole, slightly stooped shoulders and a potbelly, duck-footed, really a mess. He was wearing a shapeless gray seersucker suit, a dirty white shirt that blossomed around his waist, and a bow tie that barely held together. The glass he held in his hand contained something bright red, guess what. A clue: a slice of lime floated in it.

"Good morning, Joab," Bitsy said through tight lips that barely moved as we walked up the steps to the porch. "Why don't you have another drink? His name's Joab Wolfe," she said to me.

He finished off what he had, and rattled the stained ice cubes in the glass. "Not a bad idea. A very good idea, in fact. *Wyvonny?*"

The maid was there instantly. "Mr. Joab?" She gave Bitsy a quick, anxious glance.

He handed her his glass. "Another Bloody. Heavy on the Stoli. Ho ho ho."

"Miss Bitsy?"

"You heard the man. Give him what he wants."

"He got into it hisself, Miss Bitsy. I be out in the kitchen with Lily Dell."

"I don't give one good damn what Mr. Wolfe drinks, how much Mr. Wolfe drinks, when he drinks it, or how he gets it. Give him what he's craving for."

"You heard the lady, Wyvonny. Ho ho ho."

"Look, I've got some things I ought to be doing," I said.

Joab Wolfe looked at me as if I had just that moment materialized. "Who the hell are you?"

"None of your damned business," Bitsy said.

"I'll check in with you a little later," I said to Bitsy.

"Don't you dare move an inch," she commanded me.

Joab Wolfe reached inside his jacket pocket, withdrew an envelope, and offered it to Bitsy with a flourish.

"What's this?"

"My letter of resignation as your editor in chief."

She snatched the letter from his hand. "And don't think I don't accept it!"

"My bag is packed and in the hallway. I've called a cab."

Wyvonny walked out with Wolfe's refilled glass on a silver platter. "Oh, good. Here we are. One for the road," Bitsy said brightly. She took the glass and offered it to Wolfe. "Guzzle this down and we'll get you another one. All you want. If that's possible."

He took the glass from her hand and drank. "Ho ho ho."

"You son of a bitch. Say that again and I'll scream."

"I had it out with Crown Prince Peter last night on that floating palace of his," Wolfe said bitterly. "The prick. A prick now and forever."

Bitsy turned to me. "This man here and I put the company together after Freeport died."

"This man is a worn-out has-been with no imagination

and very little business sense, according to your son-in-law. We argued for hours on that boat last night, agreed on nothing. Among other things, now he wants to buy a big daily, big city. Quote, one with some bite, unquote. And a million business and circulation problems, name the one for sale."

"Oh Christ! I would never agree to such a thing."

"I've had it with him, Bitsy. I'm tired of fighting him, cleaning up after him. He tried to fire me last night, but I told him what I'm telling you now. I fucking quit. And I'm not coming back until he's gone. I know he's Sally Ann's husband, but it's him or me, bottom line."

"I think you win by default," I said.

"What's that supposed to mean? I don't even know who you are, buster."

"Peter's dead, Joab," Bitsy said quickly, before either of us could say anything else. "He shot himself on that boat last night. I discovered his body there this morning."

Joab Wolfe stared at her in what appeared to be total disbelief. "Well, I'll be a son of a bitch," he whispered. He fell into one of the wicker chairs and sat silently for a moment, legs spread, mouth open, staring vacantly out at Clam Pond, and looking his age and then some.

"Mr. Wolfe, when did your talk take place?" I asked.

"After dinner last night, after everybody else had gone to bed." He turned to Bitsy. "Peter got me aside and said there was something he wanted to go into with me."

"What time did you leave that boat, Mr. Wolfe?" I asked.

"How'd it happen?"

"It looks like he blew his brains out with a pistol," I said. "What time, Mr. Wolfe?"

"Christ Jesus. What do you know about that?" he said.

"What time? Think. I know you've got a couple of drinks in you, but the police are going to be asking. I assume he was alive when you left the boat."

"No. I watched him kill himself, and then I left and went to bed." He looked me up and down. "Who are you, anyway?"

"Joab, Mac's an old friend from Chicago who's helping me get through this," Bitsy said.

"Well, I wish I could say I'm sorry, but I'm not. I wish I could say I didn't hate his guts, but you know I did," he told her.

"You're not the only one, you know," Bitsy said.

I guess I was staring at him. "Hell, I didn't kill him," he said to me. "He was still alive and conscious when I left that boat. What time? I'm not sure exactly. He was drinking heavily, and while we were having words, I got into the bottle with him. Sometime past midnight, I guess." Wolfe closed his eyes and started breathing slowly and deeply.

Bitsy pulled the other wicker chair over beside his and sat down. "Did you remember to take your medicine this morning?"

He kept his eyes closed. "No, I decided to skip a day. I'm a fucking fool."

I heard the sound of a siren coming down Clam Pond Road. "That should be the police," I said.

"Joab had bypass heart surgery last year. He's not supposed to get overwrought." She took his hand in both of hers. "Think of rows and rows of peach trees in blossom," she whispered. "Sweet thoughts, precious memories."

"Also start thinking about an alibi," I whispered. "Because the police are going to have a lot of questions, and you sound like their prime suspect to me."

3

WE STOOD IN the cabin of the boat, looking down at Peter Stallings's body, which still lay sprawled on the couch.

"This is exactly how you found him?" Noah Simmons asked.

"I took his wrist in my hand and felt for a pulse. That's all," I said. "Needless to say, there wasn't one. Then I immediately called you, because I knew you would welcome a break in your boring summer routine."

Noah looked at me in exasperation. "One more word and I'll deputize you."

"Only kidding," I said.

"It's a mob scene on Main Street," he said. "I'm fighting a holding action, and I'm losing. I swear, we've never had so many people in town before." He stepped over to the galley, pulled a paper towel off the rack, and blew his nose.

I didn't say so, but I would have bet money Noah had been swimming in Pilgrim Harbor before his office found him, because his hair was damp, dark red, and plastered

3 3

to his head. The North Walpole police chief looked like a kid ready for church, except he weighed three hundred pounds, a considerable part of it muscle. He was a lawman, but his degree from Tufts University was in marine biology, and the sea, not a court of law, was his first love. It seemed necessary to his physical and mental well-being that he immerse himself in it at least once a day.

He knelt and closely examined the black revolver that still lay on the carpeted deck close by Stallings's outstretched right hand, but didn't touch it. "A .38 Smith and Wesson. His gun?"

"How the hell would I know?"

"You seem to be acquainted with these people."

"I worked with Mrs. Binford years ago in Chicago. She learned I was in town and invited me out this morning for a cup of coffee, that's all."

"This was her son-in-law?"

"Yes. Married to her youngest stepdaughter. And president of a pretty big communications company they own."

"I know the Binford family. They've been coming here for years. Looks like he blew himself away. Any idea why?"

"I get the impression Stallings was some kind of loose cannon on the deck."

"Did they tell you anything before I got here?" Noah had decided he and I should come to the boat by ourselves and examine the body. Bitsy Binford and Joab Wolfe were waiting back at the house. Noah wanted a fill-in from me.

"Stallings and Joab Wolfe had a big argument here on the boat last night," I said. "Over business. And they drank a lot."

"Hello below! Anybody down there?" a voice called from above.

"Sounds like Hot Lips," I said to Noah.

"Come on down," Noah yelled. "What took you so long?"

"That is . . . none of your damned beeswax, young fellow," Dr. Hamish Percival, the Barnstable county medical examiner, said, climbing down the ladder, into the cabin.

He was a widower in his eighties who had been a professor of pathology at Harvard Med before he retired and moved to his summer home on the Cape to live out the rest of his days. That was twenty years ago.

Hamish had undergone some sort of sea change during the summer. A one-tweed-suit-for-all-seasons man, he had blossomed of late like a fruit tree. This morning he was decked out in a Madras patch blazer, a pink polo shirt, and lime-green trousers. Top that outfit off with a full head of silver hair and a face bright red from daily golf games, and Dr. Percival looked rather like an Easter egg colored by a disturbed child. Noah and I had concluded there could be only one explanation. Hamish had found himself a girlfriend.

"I haven't got all day," he announced.

"Used to be you did," Noah said.

"What's that supposed to mean, I'd like to know?"

"It means I'm sorry to keep you from your golf game, or whatever, except I got a little business for you. Take a look."

Dr. Percival stood over Peter Stallings's body. "You really don't need me to tell you he's dead, do you?"

"Come on, Hamish. Give me a break."

Dr. Percival opened his medical bag, got on his knees, and started examining the body. "Suicide?"

"Looks like it to me. I'll be ordering an autopsy," Noah said. "How long, would you say?"

"A few hours, eight or nine maybe. No more than that." A corpse, to Hamish Percival, was as impersonal as a bag of sand, the unfeeling thing he worked on. He hummed while he made his examination, "Indian Love Call." *Can you hear me call-aww-aw-aw-aw-alling you?* Noah and I glanced at each other but said nothing. This was no laughing matter.

"Messy," Hamish said. "A gentleman would have used the bathroom. Or gone outside."

"Dr. Percival, will you stay here on the boat with the body until the rescue squad gets here?" Noah asked. "There're some people back at the house waiting for me."

Hamish looked at his watch. "See here! I have a most important luncheon engagement in Hyannis!"

"She can wait. This really is important."

"She? See here! Who said anything about a *she?"*

"Besides, it's only a little after ten o'clock."

"Civilized people take luncheon at eleven. Who said boo about a *she,* I would like to know?"

"Okay, I take back the *she,"* Noah said. "As a favor? The rescue squad should be here any minute."

"Probably guzzling beer at the Binnacle," Dr. Percival grumbled. "All right, all right, be off with you. But don't make me late. Most important."

Noah clenched his teeth but didn't say anything. Rescue-squad response time was always a big issue with him.

They couldn't arrive too quickly to suit him. Glad I wasn't the chief paramedic that morning.

"*She* indeed!" we heard Hamish exclaim to himself as we stepped off the *Comchi.*

Bitsy and Joab Wolfe were sitting in the wicker chairs on the porch, waiting for us. Bitsy was reading her morning mail, and Joab was thumbing through copies of some of their newspapers, examining, not reading, them. They both looked up when they sensed our arrival.

I took a seat in the glider. Noah stood. He was dressed in his summer uniform, dark blue trousers with yellow stripes down the legs and a short-sleeved powder-blue shirt. He looked like a balloon spinnaker on an America's Cup contender sailing downwind in a twenty-knot breeze. "You did tell me you didn't touch the body?" he asked Bitsy.

"I found him, turned, and ran like hell," she said.

"You didn't try to determine if he still might be alive?"

"He was so obviously dead. Coffee? For either of you? Wyvonny's just brought a fresh pot."

"I ask, Mrs. Binford, because some people would have taken a look and others wouldn't have."

"Then, Chief Simmons, you may include me among the chickens." Bitsy smiled faintly.

"It just always helps the state forensics people to know if a body's been moved, that's all." Noah smiled back at her. "I guess I would like a little of that coffee. It smells so good. I try to ration myself."

I realized he knew exactly who he was dealing with here, had known from the moment he received the call on his patrol car radio. These were rich, permanent summer residents who had been part of North Walpole's social structure for many years. Property-tax payers, regular contributors to the charities, the funds, and the causes, people who had charge accounts in all the stores. Not tourists, day-trippers down from Boston, not people who checked into the Buckaneer for a weekend away from the mid-August agony of New York, slurped down the thick clam chowder, and exclaimed, "Now *this* is the real Cape!" Not temporaries, people who rented a house for a summer month or maybe six weeks, brought tears of gratitude to the eyes of the speciality-shop owners with their indiscriminate purchases, and left immediately after Labor Day weekend, station-wagon luggage racks stacked high, never to be seen again. And not true locals either, not people such as Noah, whose ancestors had kept the old town going through hard times and good for three centuries, whose family names were inscribed on the modest Civil War monument and on old, blackened Colonial gravestones, half-sunken in the ground. Bitsy and her family were part of a group Noah and his friends called the God Forevers. Ask them how long they had been coming to North Walpole for the summers and they would reply, "God! Forever!"

"That *was* his revolver?" Noah asked between sips of coffee.

"You know, I really don't know," Bitsy said. "I suppose it was. But I'd never seen it around before."

"Sally Ann might know," Joab suggested.

"It's not unusual. A lot of people keep a gun on big boats like that." More coffee. "It's a new boat, isn't it? *Comchi*? I know I haven't seen her in Pilgrim Harbor before, and I know about every boat that comes in here."

"Right out of the boatyard in Bristol. Peter only brought it here yesterday."

"She's far too big a boat for this pond. Didn't he know she'd go aground when the tide went out? In fact, a boat that size is prohibited from coming into Clam Pond."

"Peter Stallings was the kind of man you couldn't tell anything," Joab said.

Noah had been waiting for him to speak out. "I understand you were down on the boat with him sometime last night."

"That is correct."

"Did you notice the gun about then? Did Stallings have it out, even playing around?"

"He did not. He and I had a business argument, but there was never a suggestion of violence."

Noah turned to Bitsy, on his best behavior still. "Please bear with my questions, Mrs. Binford. You see, it occurs to me, the boat was new, right out of the yard, so the revolver couldn't have been on it very long." He smiled slightly. "It never hurts to know the ownership of the weapon in a case like this."

"I'm sure."

"Have you had any suspicious prowlers around this summer? Threatening phone calls? Anything like that?"

"You'd think it was murder," Bitsy said.

"I'm not suggesting that. There's no evidence of any struggle. And it doesn't look like an accident, although we can't be sure of that. No, it looks like a suicide, sorry to say." He paused. "He was right-handed?"

"Oh yes," Bitsy said. "Ask anyone."

"There's a bottle of cognac. Nearly empty."

"I drank part of it," Joab said immediately. "More than I should have, which is any at all. I'm a recovering alcoholic, Chief Simmons. You should know that. And I had a lapse last night, a rather major one, I'm afraid."

"Did you drink most of the bottle? Or did he?"

"Well, I got fairly drunk. But at my age and in my shape, that doesn't take much, not after three years on the wagon. I had maybe three snorts."

"Was Stallings drunk when you left him?"

"He'd also been drinking wine at dinner, as I recall. So I'd say he was. But I really don't remember."

"You say you two quarreled."

"A knock-down, drag-out. I ended up quitting my job."

"Temporarily," Bitsy added.

"I'll put it to you both. Did Peter Stallings have a drinking problem?"

"Certainly during the last few months, I would say," Joab said.

"Peter never drank a drop when he first came to us," Bitsy said. "He didn't smoke, either. He was the perfect young man back in those days."

"A lot of people take it up later, as life closes in on them," Noah said, looking at me.

"Isn't that so true," I said, looking right back at him.

Bitsy sighed. "I think we need to tell you about Peter Stallings, Chief Simmons." She looked at Joab. "Don't you?"

"Yes. I'll be interested to hear what we've both got to say about him. Now that he's dead," Joab said.

4

🔸 S U C H A F I N E young man he was at the time," Bitsy said. "Sally Ann brought him home to me as if he were a blue ribbon she'd won at a horse show. Do you remember how pleased with herself she looked when she used to come home with those, Joab? Sally Ann was a marvelous equestrienne when she was a teenager. Her bedroom wall covered with blue ribbons and tables filled with engraved silver cups and platters."

"I remember the exact moment she walked into the office with Peter," he said. "You're right. Look what I've got me. That's exactly what her expression said."

"And before a day had passed, you and I felt exactly the same way," Bitsy said.

"Peter was one of those young men you like almost the minute you meet him. You've known people like that," Joab said to Noah and me.

"How did they meet?" I asked.

"A blind date. Sally Ann was a Rollins girl, and Peter was in law school at the university in Gainesville. The same old story. Sally Ann's roommate was Peter's room-mate's girlfriend."

"Peter Stallings was a North Florida boy," Joab said. "Little piney-woods town west of Jacksonville. Stark, Florida." He pulled a cigar out of his inside jacket pocket and stuck it in his mouth, but didn't light it.

"There's a big state prison there," I said.

"A state pen, lots of rattlesnakes, and pit-bull breeders. And that's about all, according to Peter. We used to talk about it."

"Both of you got along with him at first," I said.

"At one time Peter Stallings was like a son to me," Joab said. "I never married, never had the time. And I was an only child. Like Peter."

"His parents?" I asked. I was not an officer of the law, nor of any court, of course, but I knew that in situations such as this, Noah liked me to ask the questions while he listened. And listened, intently, while he sipped coffee and glanced around the yard. Then never forgot a word he heard.

"His father was a guard at the prison. Nothing special. Working people."

"Joab and I were both thrilled," Bitsy said. "Without really knowing it, we'd been looking for somebody to bring along in the company."

"Especially after Freeport Junior didn't work out," Joab said.

"Peter seemed perfect," Bitsy said. "He majored in business administration and minored in journalism at Gainesville before he went to law school there."

"At Gainesville University?" Noah asked.

"The University of Florida," I explained. A son of the Cape, Noah was, who started feeling a little out of touch the second he crossed the Sagamore Bridge, over the Cape Cod Canal.

"That was, good God, fifteen years ago," Joab said. He pulled a lighter from his coat pocket.

"Go right ahead. Kill yourself. You know what the doctor told you," Bitsy said.

"Have either of you ever come across a doctor who told you smoking was good for you? If you ever do, I want his name," he said to Noah and me. But he put the lighter away.

"They got married the year Sally Ann was graduated," Bitsy said. "Peter came straight into the company. And I was happy as a clam, believe me. He fitted right in, from the first day."

"We had ourselves a bright, energetic, enthusiastic young man," Joab said. "Freeport Communications was growing. We were making money. Peter and Sally Ann seemed happy."

"Those were wonderful years, weren't they?" Bitsy said. "The best, looking back. Even if my own two marriages didn't work out."

"Understand, Bitsy and I took a small-town paper and one little radio station and built this company," Joab said.

"Joab was editor of the *Coastal Advocate* when Freeport and I got married," Bitsy explained to me.

"I was just a kid, not too many years out of journalism school at the University of Georgia."

"After Freeport's death, Joab and I sort of became partners."

4 3

"My brains and talent, her money," Joab said.

"Well, would you listen to that. I never."

"The opportunity was there," he said. "Suburban newspapers are located in the profit centers of the nation today."

"So they're bringing higher and higher prices," Bitsy said. "Everybody there subscribes to them, everybody advertises, and their cash flow makes the big boys green with envy."

"We stayed in the South, in little towns. Nothing big, but lots of properties. And thanks to Bitsy's good business sense, we bought them early, at bargain prices," Joab said.

"I don't see how anybody could screw up a sweet deal like that," I said.

"Peter didn't, not at first, not for years. Let's be fair," Bitsy said. "At first he was even better than we had any right to hope for. Even you'll have to admit that, Joab."

Joab didn't say anything.

"Well, you do," she insisted.

Joab stopped chewing on his unlighted cigar, took it from his mouth, and tossed it into a hydrangea bush. "McFarland, you're in the business. You know anything about the properties we own?"

"Not really, except you got lots of them."

"And most of them half-assed when we picked them up. Some even shopping throwaways."

"Pretty bad," Bitsy admitted.

"We cleaned them up, made them respectable," he said. "We gave our local editors complete control, and they produced good local products for us. Local news readers weren't getting. We don't rock local boats. We play ball with our communities. And, of course, not a word in our editorials about race."

"I thought it was a dead issue in the South," Noah said.

"It is officially. But it's still the only issue, really."

"You just don't write about it," I said.

"Crusaders we are not, not on that issue."

"Do you win a lot of awards?"

"We aren't completely gutless. Our editorial pages are sound. But, yes, we play the game. We're community boosters."

"Well, so is just about every other small-town daily in the country," I admitted. "But I still don't understand the role Peter Stallings played."

"He was our whiz kid, our bonus baby," Joab said.

"At first he had that little office on the third floor, remember?" Bitsy said. "Nothing but a desk and a chair and a phone, not a rug on the floor or a picture on the wall. Sally Ann made his lunch every day, and he brought it to the office in a brown paper bag. So sweet."

"Peter upgraded us, brought us into modern times," Joab said to me. "Bitsy and I didn't realize it, but our markets were ready for it. The suburbs, the beltway towns."

"They were all boom towns with people who wanted an even better local newspaper."

"Most people will buy only one newspaper. If you can give them local news plus state and national, they'll buy you. Peter bought columns, Evans and Novak, George

Will, he enlarged the news holes, bought news services, gave our best reporters and editors merit raises to keep them from leaving, opened bureaus in state capitals."

"And he talked me into spending a fortune, which we had to borrow, on plant improvement, color, offset, computers in the newsrooms," Bitsy said.

"As a result, circulation and advertising went up across the board, and the value of every property we owned tripled, at least."

"I'm telling you, smart as a whip."

"He also moved us into small cable-television companies and a few television stations in medium-sized markets," Joab said. "About eight years ago he talked us into buying three television stations that were for sale for fifty-four million dollars."

"We had to put up everything we owned to raise the cash," Bitsy said. "I couldn't sleep for weeks."

"I thought he was insane at first," Joab said. "Then, when station prices went through the roof, I thought he was a genius. You couldn't buy *one* of those stations today for twice that amount of money."

"Three. Three times," Bitsy said.

"Okay, I stand corrected."

"We had an offer on Fort Myers for that much last week. Honestly, Joab, you never could add two and two."

"I'm just a hired hand around here, lady, remember? I dig and chop, you count." He pulled another cigar from his jacket pocket and immediately lighted this one, inhaling deeply and with obvious satisfaction.

"That's number one," Bitsy said. "Half your daily ration."

"Well," I said.

"I don't relish being the bitch. The truth is, he shouldn't be smoking at all."

Joab threw the cigar into the hydrangea bush.

"Now he's upset with *me*," Bitsy moaned. "For repeating the doctor's own words."

"No. You're right."

"You know you can't add anything except the scores in the University of Georgia football games."

"What happened to Peter Stallings?" I asked. "So far he sounds like a winner to me."

"He started falling apart on us," Bitsy said immediately. "But it was a fairly slow process, at first."

"One little thing after another, as the years went by," Joab said. "At first, nothing big that you could put your finger on. Bitsy and I were hesitant to talk about it for a long time, even among ourselves."

"The truth be known, he slowly drove a wedge between Joab and me."

"Mood swings."

"He would be big on an idea one day, then completely down on it the next. Or the other way around."

"It didn't happen all at once. It was a gradual thing," Joab said.

"When did it begin?" I asked.

Bitsy and Joab looked at each other. "The office was first, I guess," he said.

"I was the one who kept insisting that office of his was unacceptable," Bitsy said. "I remodeled it for him myself, a new desk, wall covering, carpet. Nice, but nothing fancy."

4 7

"It was like turning on a switch," Joab said. "He decorated and redecorated. He ended up hiring three different decorators from Atlanta. He went all the way from all glass modern to Persian rugs and English antiques and back again."

"And that bust of himself," Bitsy said.

"I guess that's when I began to lose all contact with him. Some insane sculptor from Savannah did him up to look like, Jesus Christ, Julius Caesar. With an olive wreath yet."

"The day it arrived, he said he was going to place it in the headquarters lobby. The next day he took a hammer to it and threw it in the trash," Bitsy said.

"Or he'd be out in the main office, pounding his fist on some secretary's desk one day and sending her a case of champagne the next."

"Some executives in our company, Peter would raise their salaries, I swear he would, so he could feel free to drive them even farther up the wall," Bitsy said. "A lot of them quit on us, or he'd try to buy them back with big bonuses or new Cadillacs."

"Peter went crazy on us, and we didn't know how to handle it. It's as simple as that," Joab said. "I could talk for days about his business decisions."

"Bright and in command one minute, and nutty as one of Lily Dell's Christmas fruitcakes the next," Bitsy said.

"Did his behavior affect his personal life as well?" I asked.

Again, Bitsy and Joab exchanged glances.

"Not so much the children," he said.

"He was a loving father and such a good husband for so many years," she said.

4 8

"Yes, it did," he said.

Bitsy sat with her shoulders hunched together. "A few months ago Peter told Sally Ann he wanted a divorce," she said quietly. "He said he was in love with someone else."

Comchi had sweetie, I thought. Maybe that was it. It can drive a man crazy, it can drive him insane. "It happens, they say," I said.

"A street reporter on a television station we own in Mobile," Joab said. "Or, rather, she *was* a street reporter until she started screwing Peter. He had her promoted to weekend anchor. Everybody at the station knew about it long before we did."

"Mac, she was first runner-up Miss Alabama a few years back," Bitsy said. "If that gives you any idea."

"Quite often they make nifty weekend anchors."

"Sue Alice Darling, her name is. And looks it."

"When Bitsy found out about it, she jumped into the thing with both feet," Joab said.

"You're damn right I did. Enough is enough. I told Peter in no uncertain terms he would be out on his ear if he didn't end the affair and make peace with my daughter. I know who controls the stock in this company."

"And did he?" I asked.

"As far as I know. Sally Ann thinks so. She never knew the woman's name, I don't think."

"You don't know that," Joab said.

"What?"

"That he broke it off." Joab let out a deep breath. "I was going to tell you eventually. There was a cable owners' convention in Las Vegas back in June. Peter went, re-

4 9

member? Well, I heard from an old friend. Sue Alice Darling was his constant companion there."

Bitsy moaned. "God. What a mess that man left behind him."

"Did anybody ever suggest Peter needed professional help?" I asked. "A shrink? Or a regular medical doctor? Sometimes that can make a difference."

"Peter himself did," Bitsy said immediately. "He came into my office one day, and we had a long talk. He apologized for his erratic behavior. And, I never will forget it, he said to me, Mother Bitsy, I'm not right. No, you're not, I said. And I made him promise me he'd go and have a complete physical checkup."

"And did he?"

"He went to see a doctor named Othelle Cody, who used to deliver papers for us when he was a kid," Joab said.

"A good doctor?"

"Popular. Practices now in Brunswick. I understand he has an excellent record with gallbladders. Every woman in Brunswick, Georgia, over the age of forty has had her gallbladder removed by Othelle Cody. And many of the men."

"And, of course, Othelle found nothing wrong," I said, knowing the answer.

"Peter told me Dr. Cody pronounced him fit as a bull moose," Bitsy said.

"But you never saw any written report of any kind, I'll bet."

"Othelle isn't big on written reports," Joab said. "In fact, I'm not too sure Othelle can write." He took another cigar from his jacket pocket, lighted it with a flourish, and glared at Bitsy defiantly.

"You never talked to the good doctor?" I asked.

"I tried. He told me he couldn't discuss a doctor-patient relationship," Joab said. "So I gave up."

We heard the sound of an automobile coming down the driveway. "Oh Lord, that's Sally Ann," Bitsy said, jumping up from her seat. "I've got to tell her right this minute. I simply couldn't bring myself to do it this morning."

Joab stood. "You want some help?"

"No, it's better if I do it alone, I think. Get Wyvonny to bring you some more coffee." She left the porch and headed for the new addition to confront Sally Ann.

"I'm bringing that coffee right now, Mr. Joab," Wyvonny called from behind the screened door, and a few moments later she did, smiling faintly at Joab as she filled our cups.

"I fell off the wagon, right on my ass, Wyvonny," Joab said.

"Shore did. You want Lilly Dell to make you a fried egg and biscuit? You look like you could use one."

"No, I'm fine. You've been standing inside that screened door listening to every word, haven't you? Taking it all in and repeating it to Lily Dell in the kitchen."

"I mind my own business, Mr. Joab."

"Did you hear me say I quit last night?"

"He try to fire me once a week, twice sometimes. Miss Bitsy say, Pay that man no mind. You works for me."

"Why'd he threaten to fire you?"

"None of your business, Mr. Joab."

51

"If you don't tell me, Miss Bitsy will."

She hesitated, but only for a moment. "Want me to suck him off. More than once, too."

"Well, he won't be after you anymore."

"I know that. I hear you all talking out here."

"Well, what have you got to say about that?"

"What I got to say?" She offered Joab sugar and cream on a silver serving tray. "*Adios*, motherfucker, what I got to say," Wyvonny told him.

5

THE NEW SOUTH," I said after Wyvonny had left the porch. "I've read about it in *Time* magazine stories. The new age of better communications between the races and all that."

"Hell, I knew Peter was making advances at her," Joab said. "Bitsy told me years ago. Those two keep no secrets from each other."

"Wyvonny never gave in?" I asked.

"If she did, Bitsy never told me."

"Do you know if Peter Stallings's wife knew about it?" Noah asked quietly.

The big redhead's hair was dry now and considerably lighter in color, curling at its edges. He and I had become a team of sorts, without admitting it. This was the third death in North Walpole that had drawn us together, and in the process we had become close friends. I stood in awe of Noah Simmons's intelligence and common sense. Also, he made the best clam chowder in all of New England, with milk, never cream, and salted pork, never bacon.

"Sally Ann was never told about it, not to my knowledge," Joab said. "It never got out of control. Peter simply kept coming on to Wyvonny, especially after a few drinks. Besides, God knows Wyvonny can take care of herself if it was needed."

"She's been part of the Binford family all her life?" I asked.

"Wyvonny?" Joab smiled. "Bitsy ran into her, oh, six or seven years ago when she decided to do a little reporting herself, a series on women serving time. Wyvonny's out of prison on parole, in Bitsy's custody."

"Now why was I thinking she was an old family retainer, born and raised on the plantation?" I said. "It's the romantic in me surfacing again."

"Born in Freeport, Georgia, but grew up on the streets of Detroit. Her father was a Ford assembly-line worker," Joab said. "She came home on a bus for her grandfather's funeral and drew a life sentence for killing her granny's next-door neighbor."

I whistled.

"With a butcher knife."

Noah whistled.

"She was sixteen years old, and he tried to rape her a couple of hours after the funeral. She'd served ten years and put herself through high school on an extension program when Bitsy met her."

"Is Wyvonny a Southern name?" Noah asked. "I've never known anybody named that."

Joab laughed. "Wyvonny's mother was a great movie

5 4

fan, and her favorite star was Yvonne DeCarlo. So she named her firstborn after her. Except she didn't know how to pronounce the first name correctly."

"So it came out Wyvonny."

"The man she killed, I'm told she sliced him up like a piece of hog liver."

I glanced at Noah. "She sounded as if she gladly would have done the same thing to Peter Stallings," I said.

Joab was puffing away on his cigar in utter contentment. "She didn't sound like she was in mourning for the son of a bitch, did she? Sure, if she'd got it in her head Bitsy wanted him killed. Or if he tried something with her that set her off."

"You know, I had the feeling you were dead serious this morning when you told Bitsy you were quitting," I said.

Noah moved slightly in his seat. It was like a mountain range settling in at its creation, ski slopes to come eons later. He hadn't known about this.

"Hell, I was serious," Joab said. "Peter had me so strung out I couldn't do my job."

"It's obvious you and Bitsy have been close for a long time."

"We have been. Hell, I was like a daddy to those three children."

"Even after she got remarried?"

"Both of them were barely marriages. Ron Jefferies was our county attorney. And quite a ladies' man. For a while there it looked like he was going to take over and run things." He paused. "That had me worried. Didn't quite work out that way, though."

"She told me she ran him off because he tried to push

5 5

her around. It didn't surprise me," I said. "But you were always around, weren't you?"

"Oh yes. Before, after, and during. I'm like part of the furniture," he said. "The second one was a nice-enough fellow. The trouble was his five grown daughters, every one of them a bitch who resented Bitsy from day one. No loss there."

"You two act like you're married more than most married people do," I said. I couldn't help but wonder how Joab Wolfe had felt as he watched his business partner and closest friend, the beautiful Bitsy—and she was strikingly beautiful in those days—plunge headfirst into two disastrous marriages, one after another, while she continued to maintain her close relationship with him.

"I guess we do act like we're married at times," he said. "That woman and I have been through a lot together, let me tell you."

"Including Peter Stallings."

"Especially Peter. He tried to play the two of us against each other. Then he'd turn around and pretend to play peacemaker."

"And it was more than a business relationship, wasn't it?" I said. "It was as if you both were members of the same family, as I see it."

"All bound together. Obviously I'm a recovering alcoholic. Spent six weeks at Hazelden, up in Minnesota. But it's still hard for me to stay sober, and it always will be. Hell, I like to drink, I like the way it makes me feel. So everybody walks around on tiptoes as far as me and booze are concerned. Yet last night on that boat, Peter offered me a drink, handed it to me without even asking, as if he didn't know I had a problem with it. And if he hadn't died, I guarantee you he would have told Bitsy about it first thing this morning. We got a problem. Joab's hitting the sauce again."

I looked around. Dorsey, the chief paramedic of North Walpole's emergency rescue squad, was being led through the screened door by Wyvonny. "Where the hell have you been?" Noah asked, looking at his watch.

"A big wreck down on Twenty-eight, Chief, near Bass River. I had to make a choice between already dead and dying," Dorsey said. "A bunch of Boston kids and a highway-maintenance truck."

"You did the right thing. The body's down on that boat, along with one more pissed medical examiner. You'll need a bag." Dorsey left on the run, and Noah stood up. "I'll be going now. Please tell Mrs. Binford I'll be back later." He left the porch and walked down to the boat to meet the rescue team. Dr. Percival was standing in the cockpit, shaking his fist at him.

Almost as if they had been waiting for Noah's departure, Bitsy and Sally Ann were walking slowly from the new addition to the porch, talking quietly. Bitsy had her arm around her stepdaughter's shoulders. Sally Ann seemed to be taking it pretty well, all things considered. She was ashen-faced but dry-eyed.

"Well, the worst part's over," I said to Joab.

"There're still the two children, remember."

"Where are they?"

"Visiting friends in Monteagle, it's a summer retreat down in the Tennessee mountains."

"His parents?"

"Both dead. And Peter was an only child. I guess it could be worse."

Bitsy and Sally Ann walked up the steps from the lawn to the porch.

"I sure am sorry, little sister," Joab said.

"I wondered why he didn't come home last night. And now I know." Sally Ann placed her hands over her face and burst into tears. "How am I going to tell those two children that their daddy's dead?" she cried. "Will somebody please tell me that?"

"You won't be alone," Bitsy said, giving her shoulders a squeeze. "We'll go down with you. Joab and I'll both go. We'll get the company plane up here."

"I'll see to it. Don't you worry none," Joab said. He stepped forward and took Sally Ann into his arms.

"I simply couldn't communicate with Peter anymore, Uncle Joab," she sobbed against his chest. "I had no idea he was in such a frame of mind, to take his own life this way. If only we could have communicated!"

"Now don't you go blaming yourself for one minute, little sister. That would be really the wrong thing to do. Let's rally and just get through this together."

She shook her head. "I simply don't understand. Not a word from him. No note. No warning at all. The last words we had together were pleasant ones. Last night at dinner."

"I know, I know. Suicide really is a very selfish thing, little sister. It's a horrible thing to do to yourself, of course. But it's an even more horrible thing to do to your loved ones. Poor Peter had to have been a very, very sick man, little sister. So don't you go blaming yourself. I won't tolerate it, hear?"

"Sally Ann, you are definitely in a state of shock. A state of shock," Bitsy said. "I told you that over at the new addition."

"Yes, I know I must be. It's such a horrible fact to face. Oh, Mother Bitsy, he was so cute and nice when I first met him. Do you remember how cute he was?"

"I thought he was a splendid young man when you brought him home to us."

"I was so proud of myself that he was attracted to me. I remember thinking, Why he's just *perfect.* Perfect for me, for you, and for the company."

"There you go, blaming yourself, and I won't have it," Joab said. It seemed to me that the man was close to tears himself. "Sometimes things have a way of not working out, no matter how desperately you wish they would work out. Now we have to rally around each other on this, like I said."

Sally Ann noticed Wyvonny standing there, taking it all in silently. "Oh, Wyvonny!" she cried, rushing into her arms.

"I be real sorry for you, Sally Ann," Wyvonny said, hugging her.

"Wyvonny, I can't believe this is happening to me."

"Things happen. I be real sorry for you."

For her, but not for Peter Stallings, I thought.

"Sally Ann has been a world of help in Wyvonny's rehabilitation over the years," Bitsy said.

"Especially all them clothes you handed down to me," Wyvonny said. "Good as new and fit me like I was your twin once Lily Dell took them in. I sure appreciated them."

"Sally Ann has been so kind to Wyvonny in so many different ways," Bitsy said.

"She surely has."

"I hesitate to bring this up now," Joab said. "But what about funeral services? It's something we've got to decide."

Sally Ann broke away from Wyvonny's embrace, almost as if she had been waiting to hear the question. "Peter will be buried in Stark, beside his parents, whom he adored," she declared.

"What a splendid idea," Bitsy said.

"Peter wouldn't have wanted it any other way, Mother Bitsy."

"A private burial service. I'll see to that," Joab said. "Just the family. Including the children, Sally Ann. Children should always see their parents buried, I think. They suffer at the time, but if they aren't there, they suffer for the rest of their lives."

"I certainly agree to that, Uncle Joab."

"I suppose we ought to have some sort of memorial service," Bitsy said. "Of course, every local publisher and editor, every station manager, every news director we have, would expect to be there. It would be a circus."

"Then why not have it here and also keep it private?" Joab asked. "Death is, after all, a private matter."

"Another splendid idea!" cried Bitsy, looking at Sally Ann.

"I do believe that's what Peter would have wanted," Sally Ann said. "He so loved Belle Haven. He so loved these waters."

"Then it's all settled," Bitsy said. "Mac, do you know

6 0

some local Catholic priest? I'm not Catholic, neither was Peter, but my husband Freeport was, and so are Sally Ann and all the rest."

"You don't go to church up here?" I asked Sally Ann.

She blushed, rather deeply. "I guess we declare a holiday. Like the Episcopalians. You shame me, Mr. McFarland."

"I know a guy," I said. "Terry Riley. He's the pastor at Saint John's. A friend. I'll take care of it." I thought about it. "Roman Catholics? In South Georgia?"

"All along the coast," Bitsy said. "Scarlett O'Hara's family was Catholic, remember? Savannah, Georgia, has one of the biggest Saint Patrick's Day parades in the whole nation. They even dye the Savannah River green there every year."

"I'm sure Father Riley could do it for you. Where? At Saint John's, I suppose?"

"No, not at the church," Sally Ann said. "Peter was not very religious. Here at the house, I think."

"Why not out there, on the gazebo?" Joab asked. "We could have flowers from the garden and perhaps a light luncheon afterward."

"That would certainly help with the children," Sally Ann said. "And give them a better memory of their father's passing away. I'm not going to mention the word suicide to them until they're older."

"What a splendid suggestion," Bitsy said.

"Mother Bitsy, all of a sudden I feel a little faint," Sally Ann said, reeling a bit. She placed the back of her hand against her brow.

"Oh! My goodness! Wyvonny!" Bitsy cried.

Wyvonny sprang forward. "I put you in the Red Room for a rest on the couch, Sally Ann," she said, leading her off the porch as if she were an ailing sister suddenly come down with some tiresome summer fever.

"That poor thing really is walking around in an absolute state of shock," Bitsy said when they had left the porch.

"So are you, Bitsy, in your own way," Joab said quietly. "You look like a ghost, and no wonder, what you've been through."

Bitsy looked at me. "Such a little trouper that Sally Ann was when I told her," she said. "A flinch. An involuntary flinch when I told her. Like a doe shot through the heart. My brave angel."

"You have every right to be proud of that little girl," Joab told her. "She's been through a lot."

"If we can just get through these next few days," Bitsy said, half to herself.

"I would point out to you that Chief Simmons has ordered an autopsy. Which is routine with any violent death, of course. But the police reporter for the *Cape Cod Times* is sure to come across it, and Peter was a pretty well-known guy."

Bitsy moaned. "Oh, of course. We should have thought of that ourselves, Joab."

"How long will it take? Couple of days?" Joab asked me.

"No longer than that."

"And, of course, somebody at *The Boston Globe* will come across the *Cape Cod Times* story. And away we go."

"And within two or three days Peter's suicide will be the talk of the entire newspaper industry," Bitsy said with a sigh.

6 2

"You can count on my silence, if that makes you two feel any better," I said. "And I'll ask Noah to drag his feet as long he can."

"Do you really think this could make the national news?" Joab asked.

"I think you're going to get calls, yes, probably a lot of them. Things are pretty quiet right now, and from what you've told me, Peter Stallings was pretty well known and pretty controversial." I tried to smile. "Hell, it could end up in *People* magazine."

"I would die. I would just die," Bitsy said. She took my hand suddenly. "Mac, please stay here with us for a few days and help me out. We have loads of room."

"I don't know what I could do."

"You could deal with any inquiries we might get. Act as a buffer. You know the territory. We're just small fry when you get down to it. And Joab and I are going to be up to our ears. We've got to bury Peter, and we've got to restructure the company. It'd feel mighty good to have an old and trusted friend around at a time like this. Please?"

"Bitsy's right. We're going to have our hands full," Joab said. "I certainly would be much obliged if you'd stay."

"Then of course I'll stay," I said. The fact was, I had no place else to go, and my funds, such as they were, were limited.

Joab pointed at the boat. "There they go."

The three paramedics had stepped off the yawl and, with Noah lending a fourth hand, were carrying Peter Stallings's body across the lawn to the rescue-squad truck.

"Chief Simmons said he'd be back later to talk to you, and I suppose Sally Ann and all the others," I said.

I don't think Bitsy heard me. She stood on the porch, shielding her eyes with her hand, watching the men closely. The body was in a green body bag, and they carried it holding all four corners.

"Why, poor Peter looks like a sack of hog feed, doesn't he?" Bitsy said.

6

YOU PERSONALLY OWN stock in the Old Grand Dad company? Is that it?" Nickey, the owner and manager, asked me after he had served me my third double bourbon on the rocks a few hours later that same Monday at the Binnacle bar and grill. Acting on Bitsy Binford's invitation, I had gone back to the Buckaneer to get my things, and the Binnacle was right across the street, so why not?

"I'm going through some hard times, Nickey," I said.

"You maybe, but not me. I sold this place today for a bundle. You wouldn't believe the figure, I told you," he said. Nickey was wearing a straw hat, striped shirt, and a bow tie, as were all his young waiters and waitresses. Summer outfits. He had hired a dozen or so college kids as extra help for the season.

Nickey's announcement both shocked and dismayed me. The Binnacle was the only bar in North Walpole that was open year-round. I drank beer and played darts there with my friends. I met Kate there.

"Nickey, it won't be the same place without you," I told him.

"Can you believe six times what I paid for it? Some dude from Boston who says he's going to upscale the joint. Good luck."

"Bring on the hanging ferns," I said. "Jesus. You know, state legislatures ought to pass a law. Nail up signs. *Upscaling this joint strictly prohibited.* Leave us a few."

"I had to go for it. I like it here, but North Walpole's changing, Mac, and changing fast. The whole town's being upscaled, you ask me."

"Another year and there'll be a Polo shop on Main Street. Right across from the Laura Ashley." I slid my empty glass over to him.

"Friend, you're popping doubles like they was lemonades," Nickey said. He paused a moment then blurted out, "You know, she came in here looking for you that day she hit town, Mac. Identifying herself to one and all as Mrs. Mac McFarland."

"Well, she found me after she left here. That's why I'm here drinking alone. Kate threw me out."

"See, I already figured that out," Nickey said.

Her arrival in North Walpole came as no surprise. I had been expecting her, in a way, because I always had known that, one dark day, she was destined to appear in my life again.

"Surprise!" Earline cried when I walked into the house and found her there.

Kate sneezed. She was holding a damp tissue under a nose that was red as a Disney's clown's. She had a sum-

6 6

mer cold and she looked like hell, her face white and drawn, and her blond hair stringy and unwashed. Kate at her worst.

Still, she was beautiful. Hers was such a beautiful face that even she didn't try to deny its existence, as so many merely pretty women will. She accepted it as a fact, as a gift from God, and did Kate ever believe in God.

She was supposed to have spent that entire day in bed on doctor's orders, no visitors, no work, but there she was, sitting in a living-room chair, legs tucked under her, wearing an old, faded summer robe.

"Aren't you going to say hello at least?" Earline asked. She was sitting on the couch across from Kate.

Kate sneezed again. "Yes, she is still your wife, in case you've forgotten," she said.

"Believe me, I hadn't forgotten," I said.

Let me try to lay this out: Kate and I lived together, full time, and had, more or less, almost since the day we first met the previous winter. She was a strong-willed, hot-tempered young widow whose marriage, under tragic circumstances, had never been consummated, a Roman Catholic who still clung to her religious beliefs despite our illicit relationship, and she was the light of my life.

"What the hell are you doing here, Earline?" I shouted. "What do you want? Don't say money, because you took it all when we split, remember?"

Earline crossed her legs and lighted an unfiltered Pall Mall, her brand. She gave the living room and its expensive furnishings a long, sweeping look, its lemon-yellow Stark carpeting, its overstuffed sofa and armchairs covered with Brunschwig et Fils fabric, the J.M.W. Turner watercolors on the walls. Earline had no appreciation of such fine things—her idea of class was having a Marshall Field staff decorator pay a call—but she could judge cost down to the penny. "You don't look like you're hurting,". she said.

"None of this is mine, so don't get any ideas. I'm here strictly as a guest," I told her.

Kate was the executive director of the North Walpole Preservation Society, and this house was its headquarters as well as her home. It had been willed to the society by a rich old lady who was Kate's benefactress.

Earline opened her mouth and daintily dabbed at a bit of tobacco leaf on the tip of her tongue, the way Ida Lupino used to do it. "It may not be yours, but you look like you're making yourself right at home." She uncrossed and recrossed her legs.

Earline had a great body. I've never denied that. It was what she did to it, piling things on it, decorating herself the way some of those Far Eastern cults rouge and decorate their child princesses, that was what always got me.

That day she was wearing a white knit dress accentuated by tangerine-colored scarf, shoes, nails, and lipstick. It was a cheap dress, but the real giveaway was the Timex watch that had replaced the old jewel-encrusted Piaget on her wrist. She had bleached her red hair so that now it was the color of a sickly dime-store canary. To my horror I saw that she was still wearing her wedding ring.

"You know you're not welcome here. Go back to Chicago," I said.

Earline looked at Kate knowingly. "See what I mean?"

"Why haven't you filed for a divorce?" I asked. "The money you got from me was a settlement."

"I don't want a divorce. I never did. Mac, you know that."

"You were screwing that dentist you worked for." Earline cleaned teeth, the one thing she did well. I had first met her when she cleaned mine. Long story.

"You don't have one shred of evidence to prove that," she said definatly. "And you never did. It was all in your twisted imagination."

"What about the diary I found in your bedside table drawer? Which you destroyed. On your lawyer's instructions."

"There never was any diary. No more make-believe, please. And I stopped working for Les a long time ago, not that there was ever one thing between he and I in the first place but a professional relationship. Except what you imagined."

"You wrote it all down in that diary. A little red one. I read it out loud to you after I found it."

Earline sighed and lighted another Pall Mall. "I know you think you did. I've been relating to Kate here about how you get all these things in your head."

"Are you trying to say I'm crazy? If you are, it won't wash."

Kate sneezed again but said nothing. She was sitting there silently, looking at the two of us as if she were watching a good hot tennis match.

"Kate, I related to you how Mac threw me bodily out

6 9

of my own home in the snow when I was naked as a newborn jaybird at the time," Earline said.

"It was *not* snowing!"

"Please don't shout. It was freezing, Mac. You threw an unclothed lady out in the cold. You simply do not remember, do you? You've put it out of your mind."

"I've got to hand it to you, Earline," I said.

"He'd been fired from his job, Kate, and he'd been hitting the bottle heavily. I tried to reason with him, but I might as well have been barking at the sun." She turned to me. "You're not well, Mac. I've been telling Kate here that. You haven't been yourself for a long, long time. I'm sorry, but it's true. You need help, darling."

The dog MouMou had taken emotional shelter under the coffee table. She had been Earline's dog for years, but now she was Kate's, so she was torn and confused by divided loyalties. She stood there, bewildered, shivering and whining, glancing from one woman to the other.

"It's all right, MouMou, Mummy's here," Earline cooed.

"Mummy left you in a cage at the front door for the dog-infirmary man to kill, MouMou," I said. "Which he would have if I hadn't saved your mangy old ass, why I still don't know."

"There he goes again, making things up," Earline said to Kate.

"She was going to have you killed because that dentist she was shacking up with was allergic to dog hair," I said to the dog. "You were expendable. If you get my drift."

"MouMou, angel, Daddy is telling you a horrible falsehood about Mummy," Earline said.

MouMou barked at me furiously, her dim eyes shining

with hatred. She was about the size of two pounds of hamburger and, in her late teens, was down to one tooth. I didn't like her, and she hated me. We had been enemies for years and were destined forever to be. But, give her credit, at least she had enough sense to stay under that coffee table.

"I knew you were going to be like this," Earline said. "You need professional help. I want you to come home with me."

I stepped forward, reached down, and took her hand in mine. "Come on," I said softly.

She looked down at my hand holding hers. "What . . . ?"

"Come on. I'm serious. We need to talk privately." I tugged at her until she stood. I glanced at Kate, then led Earline outside. Kate blew her nose.

"That your car?" I asked Earline. A blue Ford compact with a small yellow Hertz sticker on its windshield was sitting in the driveway.

"I'm just thinking of what's best for you, Mac," she said.

"I know you are. Get in the car, Earline."

She hesitated for moment, then did as she was told. "I believe in forgive and forget and I hope you do, too," she said.

"Well, certainly the last part," I said. "By the way, I like what you've done to your hair."

She touched it, examined it in the rearview mirror of the car, the way women will. She wore it long, as if she were still a teenager. "I don't know. I'm thinking about letting it grow back to its natural color."

"You went on quite a spending spree with the severance pay I got from the paper, didn't you?"

"No, I . . ."

"Diamond earrings. A new full-length mink coat. Another new red Corvette, I'm told. And now they're all either repossessed or pawned, aren't they? You're on the bricks, Earline."

"I really don't know what you're talking about."

"Did you have to pay for the abortion after you and that dentist split? I understand you did. Plus that stay out in Arizona. The money that creep makes, he could have popped for that. You should have put your foot down, Earline."

"Where did you hear all this? It's a pack of lies, I assure you."

"I was a reporter in the city of Chicago for twenty-five years, remember? I know people all over. When I didn't hear from you, nothing about the divorce, I called a few of them. I know a lot about you, Earline. That Bulls basketball player, for example. And not even a starter. I would have figured you better than that."

"Mac!"

"Shut up. Young married guy, two kids. You followed him on road trips all over the country. I figure you spent the rest of the money I settled on you on air fares."

"You can't prove one word of this."

"The word I get is that he's the one who got you hooked on cocaine. It figures, because he's a big user."

"I don't have to sit here and listen to this."

"Yes, you do. You've sold the house I left in your name, sold it in late May, and now you're living in a downtown efficiency apartment. The word is, the house money went for coke, too. You've become a real candy head, Earline."

She started the car.

"Leave here with one thing clear, Blondie," I said. "I want a divorce. You file, the way you agreed to, and you'll hear no more from me. And if you don't, I will, and everything I just told you will come out in court."

"Is that a threat, big, brave man?"

"You bloodsucker. Somehow you find out where I am, and you come up here and try to pull a trick like this. Simply because I'm the only shot you've got left, and you need somebody to support your habit."

"I got friends in Chicago. You'd recognize their names. You'll be hearing from me." She threw the car in gear and roared away.

"Good-bye to all that," I said to myself, but not for the first time. I was trembling. Damn that woman.

I turned and walked up the steps to the front door. Kate had locked it. I rang the bell. "Hey, come on!"

"No." Kate was looking through one of the open screened windows.

"She's gone."

"Good. Now I want you gone, too."

"You know this was not of my doing."

"I've had it, Mac."

"You must have heard what I told her. You see what I'm dealing with here."

"You've been trying to deal with it since the day I met you. Well, time's up. You've had your best shot. Now I want you out of my house. You weren't free when we met, you aren't free now, and you never will be, I don't think. I've given up on you."

"What are you going to do?" Which I shouldn't have asked.

"I'm going to find myself a nice young man my own age and screw his brains out," Kate said.

I got out of there, telling myself this was no time to try to reason with Kate, not with that temper of hers blowing at gale force. I left thinking *I'll be back,* a bad judgment call so many of us make as we stroll down life's merry way, isn't it?

I checked into the Buckaneer and got drunk after she threw me out that day, and I was getting drunk again, just thinking about it.

"Another double," I said to Nickey.

"Give me a break, will you? You already had four. See, I worry about you. I know you and Kate are on the outs."

"That's well-known around town, is it?"

"I guess you could say. You know this place, Mac."

"You ever been to Hawaii, Nickey?"

"What? Get out of here."

"Think of Honolulu with a million tourists in town. Every hotel room taken. The vendors are selling leis and muumuus like hotcakes. Every fat lady from the entire state of Indiana is there, taking hula lessons, big asses waving to and fro. Get the picture?"

"I am concentrating, trying to get it," Nickey said.

"All those nice fat ladies from Indiana. Garden clubs in Bloomington, in Gary, they have tours. You know Indiana, Nickey?"

"Never been there."

"I figured you haven't. That's where the tall corn grows.

And there are thousands of these very large Indiana ladies, as nice as anybody you'd ever want to meet, shaking
their very large Indiana middle-aged asses, learning to do
the hula. Do you get the picture, yes or no?"

"That's your last one, Mac."

"Listen to me. Honolulu's still a small town, get right
down to it. And its citizens do not give one good flying
fuck about those dear Indiana fat ladies. Believe me on
that one." I drained my glass. "See what I mean?"

"I'm thinking about it."

"Local gossip. That's all the people who live in
Honolulu care about. How much Joe Hamama sold his
little grass shack for to that Japanese buyer. Why the hula
dancer at Don Ho's is running around on her husband."

"I never been to Hawaii, Mac. I never even been to the
West Coast."

"They gossip. Just like North Walpole and Kate and me.
All those tourists over at the Buckaneer, some of them
probably a few stout ladies from you-know-where. And
who gives a shit? But I check in and boom, boy! Whole
damn town knows Mac and Kate have split up. Just like
Honolulu." I slid my empty glass across the bar, but
Nickey ignored it.

Mary Beth, the Binnacle's hostess, walked over. She
was Noah Simmons's niece, his oldest sister's kid, and she
worked there as a waitress in the winter, when there were
fewer customers and prices were lower.

Mary Beth was just twenty-one; she had a pretty face
and straight brown hair that was two yards long, but she
tended to gain weight if she didn't diet constantly. The
word on her in town was big tits, dirty mouth, no action.

The T-shirt she was wearing that afternoon said OXFORD
UNIVERSITY DEBATING SOCIETY, in Gothic lettering, across its
front.

"Hey, good-looking, you got something very large in
mind for me?" she asked.

"One of these days, Mary Beth, you keep that up." It
was only her way of saying hello.

"I think my time has come, Great One. I guess you and
Kate aren't making it anymore, huh?"

"Christ, they'll be printing it on the back of raisin-bran
boxes next," I said. "Where did you hear that?"

"Oh, a little bitty birdy told me a couple of minutes ago
when I seated her and some blond hunk two tables back
from the bar." She whistled. "What a dreamboat. That
bulge in his crotch almost made me faint. And a whole lot
younger than you, McFarland."

I didn't turn and look. I wanted to, but I didn't. On the
jukebox James Taylor was singing. Kate was sitting not
ten feet away from me, and I had never felt so lonely in
my life.

"Hit me," I said to Nickey.

"Mac, I tell you what. Why don't you go on across the
street, the Buckaneer? Drinks on me tonight," he said.

"Something the matter? Am I disturbing the peace or
something?"

"One more. And I don't know why I'm doing it. Then
you beat it."

"You spotted them, didn't you? Old friend. You truly
are a good friend, Nickey. Have I ever told you that?"

"Drink that and get on the Buckaneer, please?"

"Mary Beth describes him as a good-looking youngster

with a bulge between his legs. A hunk, I think she said."

"See, like I said, I don't want any trouble in here, even though I just sold the joint for a bundle."

The people seated at the table directly behind me paid their check and left. Now there was an unobstructed view, and I glanced around quickly, like a San Francisco private eye in a thirties Warner Bros. movie.

I felt sick. Mary Beth was correct. He was a handsome son of a bitch, a few years older than Kate, but not many. He was resort-dressed in a cream-colored cotton sweater, blue button-down shirt, khaki trousers, and white sneakers, no socks. He was coming on strong to Kate, rubbing her bare ankle with the toe of his sneaker, touching her knee lightly to make a point while he talked. The fucker. I knew all those moves.

Kate was wearing shorts and a yellow top. Her blond hair was shining in the late afternoon sun that poured through the window, and she didn't seem to mind all the attention. She was smiling at the yuppie bastard, obviously enjoying his courtship. I wanted to choke him. I didn't think she had spotted me yet.

Mary Beth hurried to the bar. She was breathless. "Two gin and tonics. They've been out on his motor cruiser. He's got this humongous hard-on."

Everybody in town knew Kate. They knew her when she was Katey O'Doul, the Irish Catholic schoolgirl who had grown up as the only daughter of a widowed hospital emergency-room nurse. They knew her as the Preservation Society's yes-or-no, the head of a generously endowed organization that threw money at various worthy causes. And they knew her as Kate Bingham, the beautiful

7 7

young widow who had allowed that down-at-the-heels Chicago newspaperman to move into the old Jane Drexel estate with her and, the word was, share her bed.

Mary Beth served the drinks to them and rushed back. "He's an eye doctor in Boston. He's talking about cornea transplants," she said. "He actually transplants eyes. Eyeballs, I guess it is."

I had drifted into town that previous winter, out of work, out of money, out of love, and out of luck, and found Kate, who, in her own way, was as lonely and as down on her luck as I was. We were a fit, a matched pair, and that doesn't happen often.

Her mother had been killed in a highway wreck. Her husband had died in a freak accident on their wedding day. Her teenage sweetheart had committed suicide. And the rich old woman who had paid her way through college had been murdered. Then she got tied up with a man whose crazy wife wouldn't divorce him. Not a great track record.

Mary Beth had wandered over to listen in, and now she ran back to report again. "He's lonely. Except for his work he's all alone. Works all the time. He just transplanted a dead friend's eyeball to another friend's eye and he cried all through the operation. God, he's sexy!"

The one constant in Kate's favor was her great beauty. She might not look like much moping around the house, nursing a bad cold, but get a Dristan into her, give her a few minutes to dry up, brush that blond hair, and put her contact lenses in those baby blues, let her get into some fresh clothes, and she could look the way she looked at the Binnacle that afternoon, not cute, not pert, not pretty or attractive, but classically beautiful.

"The town's full of tourists. A lot of free and unattached girls must drift in here," I said in a loud voice to Nickey.

"A few, sometimes. Now and again," he whispered.

"Well, if anything you think I might be interested in drifts in, keep me in mind. Because I'm certainly in the market for a fresh piece of ass!" I shouted.

"Oh shit," Nickey moaned.

"I'm cruising, on the town, and looking for a piece," I said loudly. "Maybe you haven't heard that What's-her-name, Kate, and I have split. That's over and done with, a thing of the past."

"Get out of here? Please?"

"I hear she's also cruising the town, when she should be home in bed taking care of a cold she's down with," I yelled. "Well, knowing her taste, she's probably looking for some Catholic doctor, some Ivy League asshole who dresses the part, wearing no goddam socks."

"If you wanted her attention, you got it," Nickey said wearily.

"That's the type person she's out looking for. Can you imagine any woman willing to screw a man like that?" I screamed.

Nickey closed his eyes and shook his head in resignation.

"Well, give her credit where credit's due," I cried. "She can fuck a man's brains out for him. And I ought to know."

I didn't say any more, because blue-eyed Kate my darling walked up behind me and hit me over the head with, I am told it was, a Narragansett beer bottle.

7

ⵣ **I WOKE UP** the next morning in my room at the
Buckaneer with pieces of broken glass in my hair.

I remembered being led out of the Binnacle by Nickey,
who talked me across the street and into the hotel. "A
good, clean hit and no stitches needed that I can see," he
had told me. "And you took it like a man, Mac. Never even
turning your head to see who did it because you know
who did. Word'll get around, believe me. Not that you
didn't deserve the shot she gave you, Mac, mouthing off
about Kate like that."

The minute I got to my room, I fell across my bed and,
without trying to get my clothes off, passed out, out like
a light.

Once, as a teenager hitchhiking, I caught a ride with a
bootlegger. The state patrol spotted his old car with its
back end nearly dragging the ground from the weight of
the whiskey, and there was a wild, terrifying chase. I fell
asleep.

Hell, I came close to falling asleep in a bunker in North

Korea while the ChiComs were advancing through the snowfields. With my life on the line, there I was yawning. Terrified, I get sleepy.

I slept until eight o'clock the next morning.

I showered, combed the glass out of my hair, packed, and checked out of the Buckaneer. My automobile, let's call it that for purposes of identification, was parked in the hotel's guest lot. It was an old Ford station wagon Earline had left behind when we split in Chicago.

I started the car. Its engine coughed and protested when it was started, like a drunk shaken awake on a park bench. It shivered and shook like a malaria victim when it idled, left a contrail of black smoke at cruising speed, and ticked mysteriously when I switched it off.

I drove up Main Street. I decided I didn't like the Cape all that much in the summer. Too many people, too much activity. Main Street was quiet now, but by noon it would come to resemble a shopping mall. It was hard to recognize the little town I had drifted into, fleeing blindly from Chicago and Earline, the previous winter. Now it was as if the entire place had been leased temporarily to strangers. There was a time when I thought I had found a home here. Now I wasn't all that sure anymore.

I drove around the Point, North Walpole's easternmost point of land, Cape Cod's elbow, where the North Atlantic ended, roaring green into white breakers, and where the Coast Guard station with its flapping weather warning flags and its lighthouse was located. There was a moderate morning breeze, no red flag.

I drove down Clam Pond Drive, past Kate's house, no lights, and I wondered what was going on inside, and around to the pond's opposite shore, to the entrance to Belle Haven. An asphalt road led to the big yellow house. It was nine in the morning, and I had a sick heart and an aching head.

When I parked in the driveway, I could hear voices coming from the backyard.

"Please, Lincoln!"

"Don't do you one bit of good to beg, Freeport Junior. You sound just like your daddy."

The two of them were playing croquet in the backyard. Lincoln's ball was touching Freeport Binford, Jr.'s. With a chuckle, the old black man drove it out of the far corner of the court.

"Goddamnit, Lincoln!"

Lincoln chuckled again. "Got you good that time."

I walked over to them. "My name's McFarland," I said. "I guess I'm a new houseguest."

Freeport Junior looked me over. "Mother Bitsy said you'd be arriving," he said. "Her Chicago friend, aren't you?" He held out his hand.

Vaguely handsome but considerably overweight, Freeport Binford, Jr., was a young, round-faced man who already looked middle-aged, and by the time he was twenty years older would look like the last surviving Spanish-American War veteran.

I looked around. "Where is everybody?"

"They've gone to Tennessee in the company plane to pick up the children," he said. "Polly and Cyril have gone to town."

"Your mother asked me to stay here a few days. Something like this happens, you want people you know around, I guess."

The croquet game abandoned, he and I walked across the lawn to the porch together. Wyvonny had spotted us coming, and by the time we reached the porch, she had brought out coffee and warm pecan rolls for me and a can of Classic Coke for Freeport Junior. He popped the top and took a long drink from it. "I never could stand the taste of coffee," he said.

"I'm sorry about your brother-in-law," I said. "I see that boat of his is still aground."

"The Coast Guard's supposed to tug her free today, but they called and said they've had an equipment breakdown. It's going to be three or four more days before they can get here."

"Well, your mother's lucky you're here to take care of things like that. She's got enough on her mind."

"The silly son of a bitch should never have tried to get that monster in here in the first place," he said. "I tried to tell him."

"Bitsy told me you helped him sail it up from Bristol."

"Helped him? *Helped him?* I sailed the thing up here practically by myself."

"I understood Peter was a pretty fair sailor."

"He was. But not on this trip. He begged off with a sprained right wrist. He couldn't haul in a sheet. Hell, he barely could handle the wheel. Not that I needed any help especially."

"He was lucky to have had such an expert seaman with him."

"You can say that again. One person can do it. That thing's a push-button sailboat. But it keeps one man busy."

"You two were close friends?"

He finished his Coke, twisted the can, and placed it on the coffee table. "I hated the bastard's guts. And the feeling was mutual, I assure you."

"But he asked you to crew for him."

"He needed my help. Simple. The two of us didn't get along when I was with the company, and we didn't get along after I left it. After he forced me out, I should say."

I was wolfing down the pecan rolls. I had never got around to having dinner the night before, due to my busy schedule.

"From all I've heard about him, he was difficult to get along with," I managed to say between bites.

"He forced me out of the company, not that Mother Bitsy and Joab were such loyal friends. Me, you're looking at a moron, to hear Peter tell it. I had the title assistant to the publisher, and I couldn't add two and two as far as he was concerned. Accused me of bankrupting the company. Well, I can damn well add two and two."

"Sure you can."

"You've heard of South Georgia State University, of course."

"Of course. Who hasn't?"

"I was treasurer of Kappa Alpha fraternity there."

"I can believe that. Just meeting you, that comes across."

"You try balancing that frat house's books for a year. And still have enough money left over to throw a dues-free spring beer bust. I can add two and two, believe me."

"What are you up to these days?"

"I took a buyout from the company. I headquarter in Houston now. Commercial real estate is my business. I'm in the money-making game."

"Not a lot to be made in Houston right now."

"Sure, we've seen some hard times. Commercial real estate hit about rock bottom at one point. But there's a fortune waiting to be made in it now."

"Some good deals to be had?"

"What I got a chance to pick up for next to nothing you wouldn't believe. I could swing it myself, except my goddamn ex got herself a shyster lawyer and took me to the cleaners for every cent I owned, the bitch."

"I had one of those myself," I said. "I can appreciate your problem."

"Bleed you blind," Freeport Junior said. "On top of that, she's got my ex-father-in-law suing me, for God's sake. I mean, a gentleman, I used to call him that, who I have attended Houston Oiler games with."

"Suing you? Certainly not!"

"Claiming mismanagement. The son of a bitch."

"The son of a bitch! And there you were, doing the best you possibly could, no doubt."

"I was into him, no argument about that. But I'm good for my debts."

"Why, of course you are. Just looking at you tells me that. The legal fees alone must be eating you alive." Maybe a parking lot, I thought. Just maybe he could run a parking lot, although that might be pushing it.

"There's no such thing as a cheap Houston lawyer,

believe you me," Freeport Junior said. Wyvonny brought him another Coke.

"Son of a bitch! Tough luck!" I said. No, I decided, not even a parking lot, not even an unpaved, dollar-a-day, park-and-lock parking lot.

"It's a great opportunity for the company," he said.

"Did you bring that up with Peter during your boat trip?"

"We came to more or less a verbal agreement, in fact."

"Nothing on paper?"

"No. We were at sea, remember."

"The man thought you were a moron. Businesswise, I mean."

"But give the devil his due, my friend. A man would have to be blind not to see this opening. No, I had the feeling Peter was seriously thinking about calling in his lawyers and putting Freeport Communications in play down in Houston."

"And instead, he decided to blow his brains out. Tough luck!" I snapped my fingers. "Hey, no chance your ex-father-in-law might change his mind and come to his senses?"

"Him? I tried to reason with him. The son of a bitch said he wouldn't trust me to run a parking lot for him."

With Lincoln's help, I transferred my bags from my car to the guest room I had been assigned, and stayed there until I saw Freeport Junior dump a golf bag into the trunk of his Honda Accord and drive away. Then I walked downstairs immediately, out the back door, off the porch, across the lawn, and down to the *Comchi.* My conversation with Freeport Junior had given me an idea.

I stepped on board the boat, stood in the cockpit and peered into the cabin, then climbed down the ladder carefully. Peter Stallings's body was gone, of course, and Noah, or somebody, had removed the revolver. Otherwise, things looked about the same as they had twenty-four hours earlier.

I walked aft to the main stateroom. It contained a big oval-shaped bed, and wouldn't Miss Second Place Alabama have enjoyed bouncing around on that?

The master bath, full-sized, was forward of the stateroom, its plumbing tied to the galley's. I went in, opened the medicine cabinet, and found Bic disposable razors, a tube of Gleam, Sea & Ski, Tums for the tummy, and a bottle of Alka-Seltzer tablets.

I also found Tenormin atenolol, which slows the heart beat, Cardizem diltazem HCI, which thins the blood, and Maxzide triamterene hydrochlorothiazide, which causes one to wake up and go wee-wee potty in the early morning hours if one takes it late at night.

It was what I had been looking for, what I somehow had known I would find.

The bottles of prescription medicines provided irrefutable evidence that Peter Stallings had suffered a stroke, just as I had. No wonder he had needed Freeport Junior to help him sail his almost all-electric boat up from Rhode Island.

I read the prescriptions given by Dr. Othelle Cody. They were far stronger than those Dr. Percival had given me.

8 7

I walked back into the main cabin. There was a Digital computer set up on a table in one corner, the same system we had used in my Chicago newsroom. I switched it on, remembering that I had noticed an uplink on the boat's mast, and tapped the "return" key. ENTER CONNECT COMMAND, it instructed me. Freeport Communications, I thought, typed C-FC and tapped the "return" key again. LOG IN, the Digital's screen said. STALLINGS, I typed and hit "return" again. PASSWORD, the computer replied. And there it had me. Peter Stallings had a locked file.

If you are programmed into a system, you can choose any password you like to lock and open your personal file, and if you keep it a secret, that makes it a safe depository of information. At the newspaper my password was HORACE, my real first name, which very few people knew. PETER, I typed. INVALID, the computer answered immediately.

I looked around the cabin, thought about everything Bitsy and Joab had said about him. Of course. COMCHI, I typed, and the computer's screen blossomed with operating instructions, ending with TO PROCEED HIT CMD. I did, and got a long listing of broad subject headings: NEWSPAPERS, RADIO, TV, CABLE, EDITORS, COLUMNISTS, FINANCE, OTHER . . .

I moved the selector bar down to OTHER and tapped the right arrow key. This gave me ADDRESSES, ACCOUNTS, ANNIVERSARIES, ALABAMA, AUTOS, BIRTHDAYS, BOAT . . . I moved the selector key down to MEDICAL. Now I was getting into him. Not to worry, ALABAMA, I would get back to you later.

MEDICAL gave me a list of prescriptions, numbers, and dates, and a list of doctors with their addresses and phone numbers.

The secretary in his office told me that Dr. Othelle Cody

was indisposed. So, what the hell, I tried his home. He answered on the second ring, and I could hear the sound of a television set in the background. The telephone must be in the pine-paneled rec room, I thought, on a table right next to the E-Z Lounger.

"Halo. Doctuh Cody heah," he said. Deep, Deep South, this good buddy was, from that part of the country where alligators lumber up on your lawn unannounced and gobble down your puppy dog if they catch him napping in the noonday sun.

"Dr. Cody, I'm sorry to disturb you at home," I said. "My name's McFarland. You don't know me, but I'm a friend of Bitsy Binford's."

"Wi, yais suh. Hi yew? Hi mae ah hep yew?" he answered. Water moccasins, too, I thought, and lots of them, hanging from the weeping-willow trees over the algae-choked goldfish pond.

"Bitsy is indisposed. But she asked me to call you with some sad news. Peter Stallings passed away suddenly this morning."

"Mah Gawd! Ah dew swanee! A dad-blamed ole stroke, ah jest bet yew a pretty. Ah wahned hem, dad-gum if ah didn't."

I didn't correct his false assumption. "You were treating him, Dr. Cody?"

"Yais suh, ah wuz. Thet dad-blamed old hi blud pressuh of hes wuz off thuh wahl, too." There was a day when I spent a lot of time in the South, covering the civil-rights movement in various states. Dr. Othelle Cody had, without a doubt, the deepest, most pronounced Southern accent I had ever heard.

8 9

"I was wondering, Dr. Cody. Had Peter suffered any strokes in the past?"

"None thet he'd evuh admit. Yew know hi he wuz. But, yais suh, ah thank he did, yais, ah dew."

What medical school? I wondered. Probably the one at Okefenokee State University. "We have a bad connection. I can barely understand you," I said.

"Ah'll talk louduh!" he shouted. Christ, a Rebel yell.

"What caused you to believe he had a stroke?" I asked.

"He come in heah to see me awhile bac! Said he wadn't feelin gud!"

"The connection's cleared up, Dr. Cody. No need to shout anymore."

"No wundah. Hes dad-blamed blud pressuh wuz up hi'n ah kyte!"

"Dr. Cody? I can hear you fine now."

"Gud! Ah seen he wuz having trouble movin hes ryte han, hes whol ryte arm, in fac."

"I see. That's a pretty reliable sign of trouble, isn't it?"

"Yais suh, et is."

I knew that because the same thing had happened to me. A couple of weeks earlier I woke up one morning and discovered my right arm was dead and lifeless. I couldn't make my right hand move. It scared me and, like Peter Stallings, I tried to hide it. I told Kate I had caught a cold, and I stayed in bed that morning. After she went into her office to work, I slipped out of the house and went to see Dr. Percival, who complained that he was not the person who should be treating me but prescribed some medicine, nevertheless, the same prescriptions I had found in Peter Stallings's bedside table.

Since then I had regained most of the use of my arm, but my right hand—especially my right thumb and index finger—was still weak. That was why I had dropped Bitsy's coffee cup. Also, my handwriting was almost illegible.

"He tole me he sprayned it," Dr. Cody said. "Petuh, ah tole hem, ah'm gone give yew these heah pills, but ef yew got eny brains in yore hed, yew'll get yosef to Savannah and let a specialist look yew ovah," Dr. Cody told me.

"But he never did, as far as you know?"

"Shoot, he woodn't even lay down on mi dad-gum couch and raist."

"Did you tell anybody else about his condition, Dr. Cody? Sally Ann? Bitsy?"

He hesitated. "Ah shoud of, but ah didn't. He swo me to secrecy."

I sighed. "Poor Peter."

"A sudden daith, yew say?"

"He went out like a light, Dr. Cody. He never knew what hit him."

"Thet dad-blame ole hi blud pressuh'll sho do thet to yew," he said.

8

BUBBA OLSEN stared intently at his catcher, shook off a sign the catcher had not given him, stared some more, and finally nodded his head slowly, solemnly accepting a sign the catcher had not given him.

He took his stance at a right angle to the batter and carefully checked first base, where there was no runner. In fact, all the bases were empty. He went into his windup, lifting his right leg high into the air, and threw the ball.

"Stee!" the plate umpire bellowed authoritatively, shooting his right hand up. The side was retired.

At least seventy miles an hour, I decided. Maybe seventy-five. Could that be right?

North Walpole's Little League baseball team cheered and jumped with joy and ran in for its turn at bat, and South Walpole's took to the field. The town's Little League stadium was filled.

North Walpole's catcher had no hand signals for his pitcher because Bubba Olsen had only one pitch, a fastball, but a fastball that was picking up speed and authority and becoming more accurate with each passing week that summer.

At the age of twelve, Bubba was a young giant, already larger than his father, Jimmy Olsen, who was clerk of the Barnstable County probate court. That was no big deal because everybody in town was bigger than Jimmy, including his wife, who was Noah Simmons's sister, and his daughter, Mary Beth, the hostess at the Binnacle.

Jimmy was the Little League team's manager, a position of authority and responsibility he took most seriously. He considered himself the town's unrivaled expert on baseball lore, and he would talk the game for hours with anyone willing to listen. But he was well liked because he made no enemies, had no axes to grind, and was a tough little hickory nut who screwed his fat wife in the bathtub when they were on good terms and defended himself as best he could when they weren't. When Jimmy appeared in some new cast, on a leg or an arm, or all bandaged up, everybody knew Delores had coldcocked him yet again.

I was a mighty man in Jimmy's eyes, because back in the days when men were boys, I had pitched one season for the Class A Clinton, Iowa, Giants, no need to ask about my won-loss record. At his request, I had been working with Bubba since the early spring, trying to teach him the rudiments of control, and at last there were some signs of progress. Bubba still had a tendency to throw the ball over his catcher's head now and again, and sometimes up in the stands behind home plate, but he was a sweet, well-mannered youngster who tried hard, and he was coming along.

I attended the games when Bubba was pitching and, at Jimmy's request, always sat in the first row directly behind home plate to give the boy something familiar to aim at. It seemed to improve his control.

My firm rule was no curves, no sliders. I warned him he was much too young and would ruin his arm if he tried any fancy stuff at his age. But he loved pretending to shake off his catcher's nonexistent signs, and I didn't discourage that because it probably did confuse the other side a little, and the extra time between pitches seemed to calm him down.

The stands at the municipal park were packed with screaming mothers and fathers. The rivalry between the two little towns was intense, and this was the game of the year. Both teams had good, equal won-loss records, and a championship was at stake here.

Noah Simmons walked up, eating from a box of the popcorn sold by the Sea Scouts, and I squeezed over and made a place for him. "How's your head, loudmouth?" he asked.

"It's been better. I feel like a damn fool."

"You're right on the money there."

"Kate's talked with Dede, I suppose."

"They had a chat, yes."

Dede Simmons has been described as the only five-foot-two-inch housewife in blue jeans in all of America who could replace George C. Scott in his role as General Patton. She was a very cute little woman who loved her big husband and their three young children and who ran her house as if it were Fort Apache. She was, it stands to reason, Kate's best friend.

"Kate's of a good mind to kill you, Mac," Noah said between bites of popcorn. "I'd keep well clear of her right now if I were you."

The North Walpole third baseman, whose father owned the local liquor store, grounded out to second. It was 4 to 3, end of the sixth inning.

"Who was he?" I asked.

"A young eye surgeon from Boston named Carroll. Nice guy, Kate told Dede. Sweet. Kind and gentle. An unmarried Catholic who can well afford the seventy-thousand-dollar BMW he tools around in because of all the money he makes transplanting corneas."

"Give me a break?"

"I'm giving you a little advice. Your ass is in a sling, Mac. Kate told Dede she's really interested in this guy."

"Did Kate also tell Dede she kicked my ass out of the house, by any chance?"

"She said your wife paid a surprise visit. Why the hell don't you divorce the woman, Mac? That's all Kate wants."

"Noah, I'm doing all I can. I thought we had a settlement, but she hasn't filed. If I file and she contests it, the thing can drag on for years. Now she's spent all the money I gave her, sold the house, and she's going around claiming I'm crazy. Also, she's on coke. Did I fail to mention that?"

"Well, face it, you can't ask Kate to put up with that forever. She's got to think about her own future."

"She knows the minute I'm free, I'll marry her."

"From what you've just told me, that won't be until sometime during the next century. And I don't think she'll

9 5

be around that long. You know her temper better than I do."

"Well, damned if I'll go to her on my knees, begging."

"To tell you the truth, I don't know if even that would help, Mac. She told Dede she's written you off." North Walpole was back in the field, and Big Bubba Olsen was on the mound, taking his warmup pitches. "I appreciate all the time you've spent with Bubba," Noah said. "To change the subject."

"It wouldn't surprise me to see him end up in the Bigs one day. He's got the arm I dreamed about but never had." The kid sailed one about four feet above the catcher's head.

"He could use a little more work on his control," Noah said.

"Give him time. Don't push him. He's improving."

The batter stepped into the box, and the umpire took his position behind the plate. He was our close mutual friend, the lawyer Bascombe Midgeley, and he was dressed in a well-fitted gray-black umpire's suit with a face mask and chest protector of professional quality. He had bought the outfit himself.

"I can imagine Bascombe riding to hounds. But I still can't get used to him as a Little League umpire," I said. "And a pretty good one, too."

"He was the catcher on his high school team here. It's about the only exercise he gets these days, so don't knock it," Noah said. Bascombe was portly, very portly, overly portly.

"I didn't tell you. Bitsy Buford asked me to stay with

them as a guest at Belle Haven until things have settled down for them. I moved in this morning."

"I can understand that. Old friends are a comfort to have around when there's a death in the family." Finally he offered me some of his popcorn. "The first Mrs. Binford, the children's real mother, was a friend of Mrs. Drexel, you know."

Jane Drexel, Kate's benefactress and North Walpole's richest and most socially prominent summer resident, had been murdered the previous winter, and I had first met Noah when he investigated the crime.

"There's something about that suicide that doesn't go down right, Noah," I said. "We need to talk about it."

"You mean Joab Wolfe's story?"

"No, I have the feeling he's telling the truth, more or less. It's the suicide itself."

"You mean, why would a man spend a million dollars for a boat like that and blow his brains out a couple of days after he's taken possession of it?"

"Something like that, yes."

"*Stee!*" Bascombe cried. Bubba had struck out another one, retiring the side. But a run had scored and the game was tied, 4 to 4, at the bottom of the seventh, the final inning in a Little League game. North Walpole had one last shot at it.

"Noah, I was on that boat this morning. I didn't see any posted signs warning me off. I got into the guy's computer."

"What!"

"And I talked on the phone with his doctor."

South Walpole's pitcher got the first man out, on an infield grounder fielded by the second baseman, then walked two. That brought up North Walpole's most aggressive player. Little Rocko Murphy was the son of Rocko Murphy (not much imagination there), a local fisherman and a well-known hothead and loudmouth. Little Rocko was the spitting image of his old man, bandy-legged and muscular, and he approached the plate waving and swinging his bat and jumping up and down.

"You hit that fuckin' ball outa the fuckin' park, Little Rocko!" his father screamed, his hands cupped around his mouth. He was standing on his seat in the first row, down around first base, and he obviously had come to the park directly from his fishing boat, because he was still dressed in dirty coveralls and long rubber boots.

"Dr. Othelle Cody was his name," I told Noah. "I know I was out of line, but something was bothering me."

"Out of line! I haven't even questioned the family members yet. I was giving them a few days to pull themselves together." He paused. "The doctor have anything to say?"

"Peter Stallings had very high blood pressure, Noah. And he probably had a series of minor strokes over the last few months. And he tried to hide his condition from everybody."

"He killed himself because he was despondent over bad health? Is that what you think?"

"Stee!" A swing and a clear miss.

"Keep ya fuckin' eye on the fuckin' ball like I told ya, Little Rocko!" his father yelled.

"There's something you should know, Noah," I said. "I

suffered a small stroke myself a little while back. And you keep that to yourself, will you? Not a word to Dede, who'd tell Kate."

Noah stared at me, surprise and alarm suddenly in his eyes.

"*Shit!*" fumed Big Rocko. Little Rocko had hit the ball solidly, a long fly that curved foul and was missed when it should have been caught for the out by the pint-sized right fielder.

"You're the first person I've told. I went to see Dr. Percival," I said.

"Christ, Mac, the old man's a pathologist."

"With the money I got on hand, I'm going to check into Mass General?"

"How do you know it was a stroke if you didn't get examined properly?"

"Every symptom Dr. Percival asked me about I had but denied. The other thing is, a person who has one just knows."

"It must have scared you half to death."

"It did. Makes you think."

Little Rocko unloaded on a waist-high pitch and sent the ball sailing off foul to the left this time. "Hit the goddamn ball down the goddamn middle, Little Rocko!" Big Rocko screamed in frustration. "Don't swing so goddamn late!"

"Percival's better than nobody, I guess," Noah said. "He give you anything?"

"The same medicine Stallings was taking. I found the bottles on the boat."

Another pitch, this one so high and wide that even wild Little Rocko knew better than to try for it. Bascombe signaled one ball, two strikes.

"Way to watch 'em, Little Rocko!" his father yelled. "Make that South Walpole asshole throw you a good one!"

"How are you feeling now?" Noah asked.

"Better. The feeling is back in my right hand, but I still can't use it properly. I can't clip the nails on the fingers of my left hand, can't button my shirt without a struggle, especially the top one. All sorts of little things you don't think about until you can't do them."

The South Walpole pitcher hitched up his trousers, and not a moment too soon, because they were about to fall, and fired a beauty right over the plate. Little Rocko, perhaps heeding his father's advice too well, took it, waiting for that good one.

"Stee!" Bascombe thundered without a moment's hesitation. A good call. The boy was out on a called third strike.

"Bullshit!" Big Rocko screamed in anguish. "Bullshit!"

Little Rocko, ever his father's son, started jumping up and down, waving his arms and screaming at Bascombe. The pejorative "Asshole!," cried out in a shrill, childish voice, could be heard clearly by everyone, even with all the crowd noise.

Bascombe wheeled around, and his right arm shot forward. Little Rocko had been ejected from the game.

"I'll kill that fat prick!" Big Rocko screamed, totally out of control, which wasn't all that unusual. He vaulted the waist-high fence that bordered the field and took off on a dead run for Bascombe. Paulette, his long-suffering and usually pregnant wife, struggled over the same fence, showing a lot of leg, and took off after Big Rocko. She was too late. An aggressive watchfob guard during his high school days and still a hardworking fisherman, Big Rocko tackled Bascombe around his chest, and the two men fell to the ground. Rocko, arms flying, began pummeling Bascombe.

"Oh Christ," Noah moaned. He jumped the fence and ran out on the field to break up the fight.

"I think somebody killed him," I said aloud to myself.

Rocko had his hands locked around Bascombe's neck. Noah was trying to pry them loose. Paulette, still wearing her high heels, was kicking Rocko on his back, screaming, "Unsportsmanlike conduct, you fucker!" And Jimmy Olsen was holding a crying, screaming Little Rocko around his waist, from behind, trying to keep him out of it.

"Damn good game so far," said the man standing next to me.

6

DR. HAMISH PERCIVAL lived alone in a big Victorian frame house, bought as a summer home during his Harvard Med School teaching days, years before Cape Cod's real estate prices went into orbit, and worth twenty times what he had paid for it. It was an austere house, slate gray with black shutters, with very little yard and no significant landscaping. But it was located directly across the street from the Pilgrim Harbor Yacht Club, which guaranteed steady appreciation in value.

Noah and I found him there, entertaining.

Hamish's car, a brown, spotless, fifteen-year-old Chevy, was parked out front, but it took him so long to answer his doorbell that we began to think he might be out taking a walk or playing golf. "Ah, there you are," he said, as if he had been expecting us, when at last he opened his door.

Noah and I glanced at each other.

Hamish was featuring yet another natty outfit that afternoon, red-and-white checked trousers, powder-blue shirt, a white ascot, and this, well, maroon beret.

"Hamish, sorry to disturb you at home, but Mac and I need to talk to you," Noah said. "May we come in?"

"Well," he said. "I'm really quite occupied at the moment. Perhaps I could get back to you."

"It's important. Otherwise, we wouldn't be bothering you at home this way," Noah said.

"Yes. Well, if you could telephone in perhaps two hours."

"Business, Hammy?" a woman's voice called from within the house. "If it is, you go right ahead and take care of it. I can always get on my scooter and scoot."

Hamish surrendered. He closed his eyes, took a deep breath, and opened the door wider. Noah and I stepped inside. We had come there directly from the Little League park, shortly after Noah had restored law and order. Game suspended, whatever that meant. They decided to call that one a 4–4 tie and play another one.

"My, the police. I keep forgetting your official position, Hammy," the lady said.

She was in her sixties, considerably younger than the good doctor, and her beehived hair was carbon black. She was wearing a pink blouse and lime-green culottes, but was an attractive lady with a pleasant face and a ready smile. Johnny Mathis was singing his heart out on the record player, and there were two glasses of white wine on the coffee table. Occupied, indeed. Afternoon delight.

Hamish introduced us. "Police Chief Simmons and Mr.

1 0 3

McFarland. Mrs. Darlene Steinman. Mrs. Steinman is employed in Hyannis." He added no further word of explanation.

"In medical records, in the Barnstable County Public Health Office. Where I started from scratch after my late husband expired, and I find it a real personal challenge," Mrs. Steinman said.

"We met, Mrs. Steinman and I, Darlene and I," Hamish said.

"Medical records was the miracle that brought Hammy and I together," Mrs. Steinman said. "And believe you me, that is a story in and of itself. Why don't you tell your friends about it, Hammy?"

"That is correct. Mrs. Steinman and I met through medical records," Hamish said.

"I was so nervous," she said. "I thought I never would find what he was looking for. I've told Hammy I think it was fate."

"Well, good for medical records," I said. "Darlene, you're like a breath of fresh air in this old house."

"Nothing wrong with this house," Hamish said.

"Mac means he and I both thought Hamish has been in sort of a rut," Noah said. "Occupied by his job. A heavy workload."

"Exactly what I've told him," Darlene said.

"I do find satisfaction in my work," Hamish said. "Being medical examiner for all of Barnstable County is quite a challenge."

Mrs. Steinman held up some bright, rainbow-colored folds of cloth. "Look. I'm making Hammy some new drapes for his study. It's so dark and gloomy in there. I mean, in my book, the study of a renowned college professor of pathology emeritus needs light, and plenty of it, to come through the windows so he can see to read all those medical journals he has his nose in. Right?"

"Right!" Noah and I said together.

"My study always has had ample illumination."

"Don't you like the drapes, Hammy? Something about the pattern? The colors?"

"Darlene, I have told you the draperies are perfectly satisfactory," he said. "In fact, they are quite cheery."

"He's just an old grumble grouch, Darlene," I said. "Don't pay any attention to him. He's not happy unless he's grumbling."

"He's got a full-grown skeleton in that study," she said. "Behind his desk. I call him Herbie. He looks like a Herbie to me. When he gets grouchy, I tell him I'm going to get Herbie after him."

"A departing gift from my students when I retired," Hamish said. "Given in jest, of course."

Darlene held the draperies up and examined them again. "If I do say so myself, I can sew. I brought my portable Singer over, in case the hems need adjusting."

"Mrs. Steinman sews nearly all her own clothes herself," Hamish said in a tone of voice almost approaching pride. "Those slacks, for example. Or shorts, I should have said."

"Culottes, Hammy!" Darlene blushed. "I'm far too gone for shorts."

"I have told you that you are not, Darlene," Hamish said.

"Oh, there was a day, I don't mind telling you, when

1 0 5

heads turned. When I was a girl." She was walking out of the living room as she spoke. "I'll just go and make some fresh coffee and give you men the privacy you need to discuss your business."

The three of us walked into Dr. Percival's dark study and sat in three deep dark brown leather chairs whose old coverings had cracked into thousands of tiny pieces. Everything there was fading, and the framed photographs in the bookcases were browning. The house and all its belongings had been growing older along with their owner.

"Mrs. Steinman is quite pert," said Hamish, settling himself. "A lot of company."

"It was your lucky day when you walked into medical records, I'll tell you that," I said. "You just better watch your step and make sure you don't lose her, a pretty woman like that one."

"She is quite handsome. She insisted on adding some decoration in this room. I purchased the drapery material, of course, after she chose it. I wouldn't have had it any other way."

"Hamish, you have performed the Stallings autopsy?" Noah asked.

"All done. The report should be in your office by tomorrow." He packed and lighted his pipe. "Death by self-inflicted gunshot wound. What's the problem?"

"The problem is that Mac here questions suicide. And I think he's got a fairly good case to make. I'm going to let him ask you the questions."

Dr. Percival puffed on his pipe, in his professional

mode now. "Go ahead. But I doubt if I can be of any help to you."

"Why is that?"

Hamish sighed and puffed. The smoke smelled like dried apples. "Because, boys, I'm afraid I went ahead and ordered the body embalmed." He removed his beret. "I know it was a violent death, but with all that talk on the boat, I suppose I got the notion it was all settled as far as you were concerned, Noah." He coughed. "Not quite as young and on top of things as once I was, I'm afraid."

"Not to mention being overworked," Noah said. "Nobody's blaming you for anything. And, God knows, nobody's questioning your expertise."

"You should. I have no forensic training, as you may or may not know. But at least I'm an expert hospital pathologist, which is a far more qualified person than most county coroners. Hell, some of them aren't even medical doctors. Did you know that? Nothing says they have to be."

I nodded my head in appreciation of what Hamish was saying. As an old police reporter who had read more than his share of law-enforcement journals during rainy afternoons spent in station houses when nothing was happening, I was familiar with the statistics.

There are about four hundred thousand deaths in this country each year that are violent, accidental, possibly suicidal, or unexplained. Every year thousands of murders go unsolved and scores of innocent people are sentenced to prison, or to death, for crimes they didn't commit.

And nobody really knows the number of death certificates that are issued listing the wrong cause of death. One major reason is inept medical death investigations. Barnstable County was luckier than most to have Hamish Percival.

"What's the cause for your concern, Mac?" he asked me.

"Okay, a lot of this is guesswork, based on my own experience."

"Understood."

"Did you find anything in your autopsy to indicate that Peter Stalling's might have suffered a stroke recently?"

Hamish shifted his weight in his chair and thought about it. "Well, there was not very much left up there to examine. The poor fellow did blow his brains out, after all."

"But did you find anything?" I insisted.

He smiled grimly. "Yes. I found what I suspect I would find if I cut you open, Mac. Some edema. It's all in my report."

Mrs. Steinman tiptoed into the room with a coffee tray, left it on the table, and tiptoed out again, holding a finger to her lips, not saying a word. She had included sugar cookies.

"Edema," Noah said. "Refresh my memory on that one."

"It means I found some small areas on the left side of Peter Stallings's brain, or what there was left of it, which were slightly swollen and pale in color. It indicates that blood had not properly been going there."

"In other words, strong evidence of a stroke, right?" I insisted.

"Yes. But obviously that was not the cause of death. He died from the gunshot wound and from nothing else. He was alive until the moment that bullet entered his brain."

"Dr. Percival, when I came to you and you examined me, you strongly suspected I'd suffered a mild stroke, didn't you?"

"Yes. Yes, I did, Mac. Even though you insisted otherwise. That's why I prescribed the medicine I did."

"Well, you were correct. I was lying to you. Every symptom you asked me about I had. Dead right hand, no use of my fingers."

"Oh, I suspected you were lying. That's not unusual. For some reason it's rather common for active people to try to hide the fact that they've suffered small strokes. It's foolish of them. It could be a fatal mistake unless they're lucky, as I hope you were. But they do it. There have been medical papers written on the subject."

"Shhhh . . ." It was Mrs. Steinman, tiptoeing into the room again. "I'm not even a fly on the wall. Pretend I am not here. I'm invisible. I've just brought a little fruit. And I certainly hope it'll refresh your tastebuds." She deposited a large bowl containing apples, oranges, and grapes and slunk out like the Pink Panther, saying, "Don't thank me. I haven't even been in this library. Have I, Herbie?"

"Hey, this is great," said Noah, biting into an apple.

"Yes, well," Hamish said.

"Do you remember, you asked me if I'd been irritable lately, if my behavior had been erratic?" I asked him.

"A stroke affects your brain, of course. It can change your behavior, send you spinning off course."

"Peter Stallings had been sailing a very wild and unsteady course for months, remember?" I said to Noah. "Erratic was the man's middle name."

"But, see here, there is absolutely no medical evidence which indicates that a stroke promotes the possibility of suicide," Hamish said, entirely missing the point I was trying to make.

"Isn't it true that the left side of a person's brain controls the movements of the right side of his body?" I asked him.

"That is correct."

"So evidence of edema in the left side of the brain could mean Stallings's right arm could have been incapacitated," I said. "Noah, his brother-in-law told me Stallings couldn't even sail his own boat. He said he pretty much had to sail it up to North Walpole from Bristol by himself."

"Probably not his arm," Hamish said.

I looked at him in surprise and bewilderment. "No?"

"No. You see, arms and legs are rather brutish things, easily moved here and there by commands from the brain. It doesn't take much of a brain to command an arm to move."

"There goes your theory, Mac," Noah said.

"Much more likely the right hand," Hamish said. "Now there is a fine precision instrument. The hand does all sorts of delicate tasks, and the slightest stroke in the left side of the brain can put it out of commission."

"The right hand?" I asked.

"Could have been."

"Is it possible the man's right hand was so useless that he didn't have the strength in his index finger to pull the trigger of that revolver?"

"Yes. That's possible."

"The revolver was lying on the deck an inch or so away from Stallings's right hand, remember?" I said to Noah.

"I remember. We have pictures."

"And he had been hiding the fact that he'd had a stroke from everybody who knew him, business acquaintances, friends, members of his own family. Dr. Othelle Cody told me Peter Stallings pledged him to secrecy."

"I see what you're driving at," Noah said. "Nobody would have known Peter Stallings didn't have the strength in the fingers of his right hand to pull the trigger."

"But *he* would have known it, Noah. He would have known it, don't you see? And if he were determined to kill himself, it stands to reason he would have tried to make sure he did the job right."

"Mac does have a point," Dr. Percival said. "Most people who attempt suicide don't want to botch it and end up as a living vegetable."

"He would have used his left hand," I insisted. "Noah, I think somebody murdered Peter Stallings. He didn't commit suicide. The gun was found lying a few inches away from his right hand, remember? My theory is that somebody who didn't know about the stroke placed it there after he killed him."

"Hamish, did you find any trace of gunpowder on his left hand?" Noah asked.

"I am chagrined to say I didn't test for it."

"Could you take another look?"

"Any trace of gunpowder would have vanished when the body was washed," Hamish said. The old man was blushing with embarrassment. "And with the body embalmed, almost any evidence discovered afterward would be of no worth in a court of law. As you know."

"There's no evidence to indicate someone else, some stranger, was involved, is there?" I asked.

"No, not so far," Noah said.

"Which means somebody in the family, doesn't it?" I said. "Somebody in that house. One of them."

Hamish sighed. "A family affair. It so often comes down to that after all is said and done, doesn't it? Not savage intruders. Not masked men, escaped convicts, dope fiends. All the stuff of popular fiction. No, so often it's loved ones killing loved ones."

I turned to Noah, which usually was what I did when I was fresh out of ideas. "So where do we go from here?"

"The truth? Damned if I know. You've got the run of the place, remember, not me."

"Sure, I'll poke around," I said. "But if my theory is correct, I don't think I'm going to like what I find."

"I've got a feeling you're right," Noah said, not smiling, looking at me solemnly.

Mrs. Steinman was standing in the doorway with a platter held before her. "What about some chocolate cake?" she cried.

10

I'VE BEEN COMING here since I was an infant, and I can tell you, it simply would not be summer in North Walpole without this!" Polly Binford Theobald said, spearing a bite of the lobster au gratin Wyvonny had served us. Dinner had begun with a Bibb lettuce salad and tiny raw clams served with a Creole hot sauce.

"Delicious," I agreed quickly. My admiration for the unseen Lily Dell knew no bounds.

"I'm hardly a Georgia booster, God and its governor knows. But I will say this. You can't beat Georgia shrimps. Best in the entire world," she said. "Crabs, I can't tell the difference. I think crabs are just crabs."

Bitsy had told me Polly was forty-two years old, but she looked ten years older, with a prematurely aging face that matched her baby brother's. Her face looked like a candle that had burned in a drafty room, melting down quickly and undergoing vast change in the process, and she had dyed her hair burnt orange so that she looked like a fat tallow candle burning in the wind. She was even more overweight than Freeport Junior, and in an unsuccessful effort to hide this fact, that evening she was wearing a vividly colored muumuu, mustard yellow with overlying chartreuse palm froids, which enveloped her. Indeed, Polly Theobald was quite a piece of work.

We were in the dining room at Belle Haven, sitting at one end of a long, claw-footed mahogany table, eating by candlelight and drinking a reasonably good dry white wine put up by a Georgian vintner. "Believe it or not, there are such," Polly had said when she offered it.

There were only the three of us, Polly, her husband, and me. Freeport Junior was not there, although I had been offered no explanation for his absence. Cyril Theobald was eating a huge green salad and had a faraway look in his eye, as if he were wishing he were someplace else, and maybe he was. He had yet to utter his first word at the table that evening.

He was a short but very muscular man, inches shorter than his wife. Imagine a tall and gawky, overweight Jeff standing beside a muscle-bound, pumped-up Mutt. He was wearing ragged shorts, clodhoppers, a blue work-shirt, a Gucci belt, and a gold Rolex wristwatch, and he needed a haircut so badly he had to have known it. So far he hadn't looked up from his graze.

"Have you heard from your mother?" I asked Polly.

"She called. Weather's got them socked in in Chattanooga. They're overnighting. All's well, I gather."

Until that evening, when I returned to Belle Haven from Dr. Percival's home, I had never laid eyes on Polly Theobald, yet she had greeted me as if we had known each other for years, taking our acquaintance for granted.

"Did you speak with Sally Ann? How's she bearing up?"
I asked. Good manners, my mother taught me. When
you're out of money and out of luck and out of town,
that's all you'll have left.

"Oh yes. If you knew my sister well enough, you'd know
she had to chatter away," Polly said. " 'I thought the children looked simply darling when we met them at the
airport,' " she said, mimicking Sally Ann's voice fairly well.
" 'I had called Isabel at Monteagle and told her to put
Petey in his blue Florence Eisman playsuit and Mary Mar-
garet in that white blouse and that cute navy-blue jumper
I got her at Sea Island last Easter.' Excuse me. I'm sorry.
But do you mind?"

"I guess she's bearing a pretty heavy load right now,"
I said. Good manners is a reflection of your upbringing,
my mother told me. When people observe your good
manners, Horace, they will always say to themselves,
what nice parents that young man must have. Honor your
mother and father through your good manners.

Polly was on a roll. " 'And they took the news of their
father's death so well, the brave little souls. I told them
Daddy has gone to heaven. And you know, I do believe
they think he's off on another business trip of some sort.' "

"Well," I said. "If I had children of my own, I really don't
know what I would say at such a time." Good manners,
Mom said, are unobtrusive. People should always remember good manners afterward, not while you are practicing
them. I was trying.

"Daddy's up and gone to Heaven, Alabama. It's a sub-
urb of Mobile!" Polly said, and shrieked. "Don't you love
it?"

I concentrated on my lobster.

"Oh, come on, everybody in the family except Sally Ann knows about Miss Second Place Alabama," Polly said. "Just about everybody in the company, too, for that matter. Word gets around, especially in a communications business."

"I understand you don't live in Freeport," I said. "Do you play an active role in the company?" Quite often, Horace, simply changing the subject can work wonders.

"I'm on the board of directors, so-called. Not that it means a damn thing. Rubber stamp. Nobody listens to me, and never did. Least of all the late, lamented Peter. No, Cyril and I are New Yorkers. He's the novelist, of course."

"Of course," I said. My mother would have given me a pat on my cheek.

"You've read him then?"

"Oh, of course."

"Cyril's career is just beginning. He's a slow, careful writer. But one day he'll win the Nobel Prize."

There was a copy of his novel, *Down and Dirty,* on the bedside table of my guest room. The book jacket said it was his first published work. It also said he was a graduate of the Newark (N.J.) public-school system, a former blue-collar working man who had held a variety of dreary jobs, a former drug addict, now a strict vegetarian and a physical-fitness enthusiast. I hadn't cracked the book. What did he have to say to me? I also wondered about his name. Last I knew, Newark wasn't producing a lot of Cyril Theobalds.

"New York's too expensive for my blood," I said.

"A writer simply must live there these days if he's going

1 1 6

to break through. It's a fact of life. That's where the editors and the agents and the critics are, the ones that really matter. You really can't keep in touch by telephone. There must be a constant give and take, communication."

"I've heard that," I said. Stand on your principles, of course, Horace. That's the sign of a man. But sometimes it really doesn't compromise you to agree when you disagree, if it's something small.

"You are looking at a towering genius when you look at Cyril, for your information," Polly said. "I am devoting the rest of my life to the advancement of his career."

"He certainly looks fit," I said. "I don't know if I would call him *towering*." Ah, shit. Sorry, Mom. Old Cyril was five-five, maybe five-six.

"My husband could break you in half with his bare hands," Polly said.

The big salad apparently was to be Cyril's only course for the evening, and he was eating it as if he were some vegetable-starved Russian refugee fresh in from Siberia who didn't understand English. And who intended to remain silent.

But no. "You should have seen me," he said. After reading that book jacket, I had expected a rough voice, not the low and soft one I heard. "A skinny little turd until I started working out."

"What inspired you?" I asked.

"Self-revulsion. I looked into a mirror one day a couple years ago and said to myself, You can do better than this. Damn it, Cyril, you can do better."

"I read on your book jacket you were hooked on drugs at the time," I said.

"Hooked? Shit, man, I was an addict. Cross-addicted. Name it, I swallowed it, smoked it, or shot it."

"A sense of self-revulsion isn't enough to make most people stop. I congratulate you," I said.

"I wanted some respect," he said. "You're a big fucker. I'm a short fucker. Short, you got to get developed to get any respect."

"Cyril competes," Polly said proudly.

"Weights. Five years younger I could have made the Olympics. Ah, God, how it feels, being one with your body and your mind. I'm a veggie, you must have noticed. Haven't been near red meat for three years. And I dropped chicken and fish both a year ago. I'm a cleansed man."

"I'll say this, you look great," I said.

"Thanks. You don't, especially. You get any exercise at all, McFarland?" Cyril asked.

Oh, wicked tongue, stay inside Horace's mouth for his mother's sake. I hate exercise, and I don't completely trust people who like it. Either they drop dead from over-exertion or they end up looking like Cyril Theobald, pumped-up and grotesque.

I do a few morning push-ups and knee bends when conscience compels me, but mostly I walk, not because I enjoy struggling out of a comfortable bed at sunrise and making the rounds, but because I realize a man my age turns to flab and breathlessness if he doesn't make himself do it. So I do it, I walk, but I do not enjoy it, damn it.

"I walk," I told Cyril.

"You ought to be running. Walking's better than nothing, but not by much."

"Running, that way lies death for the likes of me," I said. "I'll leave that to young horses like you, Cyril." Okay, Mom? So off my back.

Wyvonny came in, bearing a big dish of peach cobbler. Cyril waved his offering away furiously, of course. Fool that he was.

"Mr. Baby going to be wanting us to save supper for him?" Wyvonny asked Polly.

Polly threw up her hands in surrender. "Your guess is as good as mine, Wyvonny. You know that one comes and goes as he sees fit. I gave up trying to track him years ago."

"Mr. Baby?" I asked.

"Freeport Junior. That's been Lily Dell's name for him since the day he was born. And a fitting name it is. Our family playboy, business genius, and all-around fuck-up. Firing him from the company probably was the last good decision Peter Stallings ever made."

"I gather the two of them never got along," I said.

"Spare me, please," Polly said. "Mother Bitsy had given Freeport Junior some fancy made-up title and a big expense account. It was like giving Dennis the Menace his own private mudhole in the living room to play in. First day on the job, he announced he needs his own private plane to zip around in. That was in addition to the King Air the company already owned, mind you. Within a month, every station manager, every local publisher we have working for us, was on the phone, saying it was either him or them."

"Which gave Peter the opening to get rid of him," I said. "Any good manager would have seized it."

"Mother Bitsy went along with it. Eventually the blessed company always comes first with her. She paid Freeport Junior off to get him out of the way. But she still, until this day, thinks of him as that poor little boy who's just lost his daddy and is afraid and trying to be grown-up at the same time. Freeport Junior plays that role well. That's what he's doing now, trying to weasel more money out of her. And he might succeed. He usually does."

"He told me he's in commercial real estate in Houston. He thinks Freeport Communications ought to invest in one of his deals."

Polly hooted. "Freeport Junior's full of it, as usual," she said. "I've done my homework on this. I talked to Houston. His wife is asking for a huge divorce settlement. Her father is suing him for the money he loaned him. Freeport Junior lost all the money Mother Bitsy gave him buying real estate he couldn't hold on to. Now he's got huge debts and angry creditors after him. And he's scared shitless because there's a chance, and a fairly good one, that he could end up in jail this time."

"Would Bitsy allow that to happen?"

"No. In the end she'll find a way to bail him out. As usual."

"I told you, Polly. He'll spend it all if she lets him," Cyril said.

"Cyril thinks Freeport Junior is going to put us all in the poorhouse sooner or later." She patted her husband's hand. "Don't worry, baby. This time my foot comes down."

"I gather he's going to want quite a lot this time," I said.

Another hoot. "Ha! I asked him that very question. He

said twenty-five. Rich Texas cowboy talk. Don't you love it! The absolute dolt."

"Twenty-five."

"I'm not talking about twenty-five cents, friend. Mr. Baby does not deal in nickels and dimes. Twenty-five million. Can you imagine?"

"You sound as if you're going to fight him."

"If Peter were still around, I wouldn't have to. But Peter's not around, is he?"

"You and Peter got along?"

Another hoot, the best yet, followed by a semi-hoot.

"Peter hated Polly's guts," Cyril said.

"Not that the feeling wasn't mutual," Polly said. "That crazy son of a bitch."

Wyvonny came and served coffee and, after I nodded, poured me a cognac from a heavy cut-crystal decanter.

"Just before she left for Tennessee, Mother Bitsy announced to us all that she was resuming command of Freeport Communications," Polly said. "A clear warning to me to keep quiet and mind my own business."

I sipped my coffee and kept quiet.

"Guess what Sally Ann said to that? 'As well you should, Mother Bitsy. We truly need an experienced hand on the helm while we're in these rough seas.' Christ!"

"Well, Polly, it's none of my business, but I don't know that Bitsy had any other choice," I said.

"Except she said *temporarily*. It may well become your business." Polly was still drinking her wine.

"I truly don't know what you're talking about."

"I've heard my mother talk about you all my life, it seems. What a wonderful reporter you are. Were you two lovers once? I wouldn't doubt it. I do know she admires and respects you as she does few other people."

"We were very close for a while there."

"I think she's going to ask you to come to work for her, McFarland. To help her run the company," Polly said.

"I don't think so," I said. "I'm just a reporter, not a publishing executive. She knows that. Besides, she's got Joab Wolfe."

"Joab's a hired hand when you get down to it. What Mother Bitsy says goes. It always did, until Peter Stallings came along. No, she wants you on board. I'd bet on it."

"Hummm," I said. Visions of perquisites swam in my head. I'll admit it. Was there ever a newspaper reporter who didn't secretly believe he would make one hell of a newspaper executive? Editor, publisher, deputy publisher, Deputy Dawg, whatever. The only thing was, Bitsy hadn't given me even the slightest hint that this was what she had in mind. "Hummm," I said again.

"If she does offer you the job, I pray to God you'll turn her down," Polly said.

I just stared at her. She was wolfing down peach cobbler and chasing each bite with a big gulp of wine. The light from the candles on the dining table made her look as if she were participating in some satanic cult, eating little puppy dogs and drinking blood.

"Care to tell me why?" this tough and street-smart reporter asked.

"Because I think we should sell the company, and I think it's in Mother Bitsy's best interests if you help me persuade her to do so," she said, wiping her mouth.

"It's really none of my business," I said, relieved to

have a quick and easy reply. "And I'm sure Bitsy would resent it if I tried to stick my nose into the matter. It's been a long time since she and I even laid eyes on one another, Polly."

"The deal is, Sally Ann, Freeport Junior, and I each own twenty percent of the company stock, Mother Bitsy the rest. But she controls ninety percent of it through a non-voting trust Daddy set up when all of us were still in diapers."

"Simple. Just sell your share."

"Not so simple. Under the terms of incorporation I can't sell it just like that. And it's not General Motors, after all. It's family-owned, and Mother Bitsy would fight to her death to prevent any outsider from owning part of it."

"What do you estimate the company's worth?"

"On today's market? I shopped it around quietly. About a half-billion, close to it."

"Jesus Christ! I had no idea," I said. "That truly is a lot of money."

"The thing is, there'll never be a better time to sell than right now, according to the market experts I talked to. The media market's red-hot. We don't own a single property that's not making money hand over fist. And, even with you in the mix, Mother Bitsy really is too old to take over active management again."

I sipped my cognac, thought, and decided to hell with all pretense at good manners. "Besides which, you want your hands on your twenty percent of that half-billion."

"You're damned right I do," she said immediately. "Mother Bitsy's kept all three of us on allowances all our lives, as if we were schoolchildren."

"I'm sure she'd say she's been buying new properties, making capital improvements. And I have a hunch the company's worth really shot up only in the last few years."

"And I don't give a damn," Polly said bitterly. "I'm an heiress worth millions and millions, and we're living in a one-bedroom apartment on the West Side. And I'm not getting any younger, I might add."

She had a point there. "Would Sally Ann agree?" I asked.

"Are you kidding? Sally Ann's in Mother Bitsy's pocket. All she cares about is her social position back in Freeport, being the young grande dame of the town. Sally Ann's been middle-aged since she was a teenager."

Wyvonny had left the coffeepot on the table, a ton of antique silver. When I tried to lift it to refill my cup, my right hand rebelled, and I would have dropped it if I hadn't quickly steadied it with my left hand. The effects of a stroke do linger on. "I guess when there's a death and so much money is involved, the survivors are bound to disagree over what to do next."

The Queen of Hoots let out another one. "Peter! Peter was a loon. Why not say it? He and I never got along, even before he went loco. Which he did. Even before he started fucking Sally Ann over royally with Miss Second Place Alabama."

"But, even crazy, he didn't want to sell your company, did he? His death certainly opened an unexpected gate of opportunity for you, didn't it?"

"What is that supposed to mean?"

I didn't answer her, because I didn't exactly know what to say.

"Look, McFarland, selling this company would benefit every single one of them, not just me. Especially Mother Bitsy."

"And what if she doesn't agree? And I don't think she will. What do you do then?"

Polly finished the last of her Georgia wine. "The company's stock prices are ridiculously low. Did you know that?"

"As I understand it, Freeport Communications is a wholly family-held company. What it's really worth is nobody else's business. There's no outstanding stock, so there can be no threat of any kind of hostile takeover."

"I'm not talking about a hostile takeover," Polly said. "I'm talking about a hostile sellout."

"But you're blocked by the terms of incorporation."

"I've talked with a lawyer. A good one. Wall Street. Mother Bitsy can't offer me five cents a share for my stock and tell me to take it or leave it. She's got to offer me something approaching a fair price or I can take her to court."

"And you're going to tell her you're prepared to do that? Good luck," I said.

Cyril, at long last, had finished his salad. Scores of lambs and dozens of rabbits could have lived for months on what he had consumed. He burped. "The big problem is, the company's incorporated in Georgia, and the stubborn old bitch could keep it tied up in the courts for years down there," he said. "There's no reasoning with that woman. How many times have I told you that, Polly?"

11

THERE MUST HAVE BEEN twenty-five workers, roofers, carpenters, plumbers, electricians, all over St. John's parish school.

Its renovation, funded by a big grant from the North Walpole Preservation Society, was in full swing, and not a day too soon. The old black granite building was in such a state of ill repair that there had been serious thought given to closing its doors until Kate Bingham opened her golden checkbook. A devout Catholic herself, and a graduate of St. John's, she had insisted that the society's name not be associated with the grant, and its parish priest, a South Boston Irishman named Terrance Riley, had readily agreed. Those who asked were told the money had come from Yoko Ono, whose name was frequently mentioned in prayers.

Terry Riley had a quick wit, a first-class mind, a clear eye, and a sure knowledge that St. John's was the end of the line for him. He was a big guy, a little bigger than yours truly, a lot stronger, and a few years younger, who once had been a starting center on the Holy Cross basketball team. He was the best cook I knew, and his rectory kitchen was a hideaway, a retreat, for me, a place where I could feed my face, wonder aloud about my future, confess my secret doubts and insecurities, and not be told to seek professional help.

That morning I found Terry sitting on the front lawn of the schoolyard, watching the work in progress. He was wearing shorts and a Holy Cross T-shirt, he was holding a megaphone in his hands, he was sitting in a wheelchair, and he had a big cast on his left leg.

"Make it snappy and interesting," I said to him. "I hate drawn-out medical stories."

"Ah, Mac. An unfortunate accident. Broke my leg. And doesn't that new roof look solid, though? It'll last for centuries, I'm guaranteed."

"What happened?" I asked.

"I fell off the roof of the school yesterday."

"What were you doing up there? Making yourself available for spiritual counseling with the roofers? Or were you up there trying to tell them how to do their job?"

"Not too hard on me, now. You know my heart's in this place." Terry Riley smiled. "One of those guys up there told me it's a good thing I slipped and fell, because he was about to push me."

"I'm sure it's a simple fracture, Terry, because only a really simple guy would climb up on a roof where he doesn't belong, and then fall off."

"I simply wanted to be sure everything's done right."

He raised the megaphone to his mouth. *"Good, boys, good. It's looking good. Beautiful!"* He turned to me. "The construction foreman gave me this."

"A brilliant man," I said. "He'll go on to build skyscrapers in the developing world. Remote places. North Barneo. The Ivory Coast. Because he knows how to deal with pushy priests who want to call all the shots."

"I do have a responsibility here, Mac."

"You also have every construction worker in all of Barnstable County who's Catholic taking time off to work here. You think they don't know what they're doing? You think those guys up there want that new roof to leak? They all got kids in school here."

"I also have other things on my mind, Mac." Riley placed his megaphone down and turned to face me. "I'm troubled."

I knelt beside his wheelchair. "What kind of trouble? What's up? What can I do?"

"They want to transfer me out of here."

"Well, tell them to go fish." I was stunned.

Terry smiled. "That's not exactly the way it works in the union I belong to."

"When?"

"By the first of the year, I'm told."

"Where? It's not like they can ship you off to the boonies. North Walpole *is* the boondocks."

"No. Boston. Cathedral of the Holy Cross."

"Cathedral? Cathedral? That's big-time religion, right? That's not exactly your little red church in the wildwood, is it?"

"I suppose not."

"I mean, that's world headquarters in the Boston Catholic tree house, right? In a word, it's a promotion, isn't it?"

"You could look at it that way, I suppose."

"Then get a smile on your face, Terry. Let me see some of that monsignor look. They're going to make you a star." I didn't want him to leave. The little town wouldn't be the same without him for me. But I was trying to put the best face on it. First, Nickey at the Binnacle, and now Terry at St. John's. Not to mention the fact that the love of my life had thrown me out on my ear for some eyeball doctor more or less her own age, her own religion, and more or less a hundred times more successful than ever I would be. And now Terry, too! Too much.

Riley looked at me. "I've come to like this town, Mac. The friends I've made. You especially. I really think of North Walpole as home now."

"Boston's your home. Besides, you've got to take the new job, haven't you? No choice, really?"

"Yes. But I'll be lost, Mac. Only one of many at the Cathedral."

"One of a very select few, I'm sure."

"No. You don't understand. You're not even Catholic. All these young theological superstars, you see. Father Darcys in the making. And all these theological bureaucrats, bishops in the making, many of them."

"And then there's you?"

"Me. South Boston. Irish ethnic, accent and all. Holy Cross and all. Priest of the people in the Cathedral. Quote a little Manley when I marry the rich contractors' sons and daughters. And didn't Father Riley perform a beautiful high-mass wedding for us, Daddy? And thank you again for the Priscilla of Boston wedding dress. I swear my own daughters to come will be married in it. And then bury the brides' fathers with my familiar Southie accent rising over their bones. Mr. Continuity with a touch of that education, sophistication, to lend a little class. That's my future, Mac. Priest to the Southies who've risen to the upper-middle class. My destiny."

"Everybody's leaving. What am I going to do when winter comes? Have you told your congregation yet?"

"My parishioners? Heavens no. Don't speak a word of this to anyone, Mac. So far I've only told you and Kate."

"Kate knows?"

"I felt she should, especially after making all that money available for the school restoration."

"What was her reaction?"

"She didn't talk to you about it, Mac?"

"She doesn't tell me everything about her business." I realized that Terry knew about Kate and me.

"She was at the eight o'clock yesterday morning. I told her afterward. Her reaction? No big deal. It seemed to me her mind was on other things."

"I see," said Old Faithful, with heart leaping.

"That was a nice young man she brought to the eight o'clock, that young Dr. Carroll. A new friend of hers, she informed me, and a graduate of Georgetown University Medical School, probably the finest in the entire country, if not the entire world, with the possible exception of Harvard Med, of course, where he learned cornea surgery. The young man's a Bostonian, you know. Of course. You must know that. And didn't he tell me his own two parents were married at Holy Cross by old Cardinal Cushing his very own self? Which must have been quite a wedding. I mean, Cushing didn't exactly take up his precious time marrying riffraff, did he? Oh, no. So probably from a formidable family. So what the hell's going on with you and Kate, Mac?"

"Terry, you remember that wife I've got out there somewhere? Earline by name? Remember her? Well, she showed up here in North Walpole. At the house. Where I no longer reside. Kate threw me out. In a nutshell."

Terry Riley sighed. "Ah, well, it's not like two of my favorite people in the entire world have split up. Nothing like that at all."

"There's nothing I can do. My hands are tied. Earline, well, sounded a little crazy to me, trying to pretend that what happened never really happened. Trying to pretend that I was nuts, or something."

"I'm sorry to say there's a little more, Mac."

"What?" He didn't have to say it was bad news.

"A telephone call from this cornea transplanter."

"Saying?"

"Asking, Mac. I'm afraid. Asking if I'd be available to celebrate a marriage in the early fall. I'm afraid."

"Kate?" I was dumbfounded.

"No, you damn fool. Jackie Onassis."

"Kate?" I asked again.

"You've lost her, Mac. My friend."

"Has she talked to you about it? I mean, she raises holy hell about the Catholic Church all the time, but she trusts you. She must have talked with you. What did she say, damn it?"

"No, she didn't. But I know her. So do you. Stubborn.

131

And principled. Even when she knows what she's going to do will make her unhappy. Stubborn to a fault. And that temper!"

"Yes, I know her. Ah, God, Terry, I know her too well."

"So what are you going to do?"

"I don't know. What can I do? Give the bride away? Shit. Excuse me."

"Where are you hanging your hat? I'm told you were at the Buckaneer but moved out."

"Fucking Honolulu," I muttered.

"Sorry?"

"Nothing. I'm staying out at Belle Haven. You know the place? The Binford people. Surely you know what happened?"

"I know the family. They're Catholic, you know. Not that I ever see any of them at Sunday mass. Quite a few of the early Southern settlers were Catholic. But I fear the Binfords' original faith has been leached out by time—that and small-town circumstance."

"I've got to say, I don't see any of them counting their rosary beads," I said.

"Pink for the girls' rest rooms! White for the boys'!" Riley shouted through his megaphone. The plumbers were unloading new commodes and lavatories. "Sorry," he said to me.

"Lapsed or not, they'd like you to say a few words at a memorial service for the son-in-law. But I don't know now, with your accident."

"Hey? This old Holy Cross center? I served mass this morning, my friend."

1 3 2

"Bitsy Binford's an old Chicago newspaper friend of mine," I said. "I'm trying to help out, is all."

"If you could pick me up and give me a ride over there? The fact is, I'd like to do it for Lily Dell's sake, if nothing else. I've talked with her about the death."

"Lily Dell the cook?"

"She's also the only real practicing Catholic in the entire family," Terry said. "She and her mother and her grandmother before her. Born to it. Talk about never missing Sunday mass."

"You know, I've never laid eyes on her," I said. "She's a presence in the kitchen is all I know."

"Lily Dell's a presence, all right," Terry said. "Among other things, she's my adviser on southern cooking. Have you ever had the honor of being offered one of her pecan rolls? She brings some in for me now and then."

"Melt in your very mouth," I said. "You say she talked to you about Peter Stallings's death?"

Terry Riley smiled. "Lily Dell talks to me about everything. I swear to you, her confessions ought to be published by some southern state university press."

"I guess she doesn't know many people up here, even after all these years of coming here," I said. "God knows there aren't many black people in North Walpole."

"Belle Haven and St. John's, those are the only two places here she does know. She never misses Sunday mass. She cooks for our bake sales. I can't make pies like that, and I don't know many others who can. And she loves bingo. Old Mrs. Galway picks her up and brings her in every other Tuesday night."

"Lincoln too?"

"Mac, I've never laid eyes on Lincoln. Never Lincoln. Lincoln's AME. Lily Dell's been trying to convert him for years. But she knows she never will. That's the only thing they differ on. And, according to Lily Dell, Lincoln never goes to church."

"His declaration of individuality, I guess. There's a young maid. Wyvonny."

"I know her," the priest said. "Beautiful woman. Sometimes she comes to church with Lily Dell. To keep her company, I think. I know all about Wyvonny, too. She's like a sister to Bitsy Binford, who tells her just about everything, I gather. And she's really like a granddaughter to Lily Dell, to whom she tells everything."

"Lily Dell, who tells you everything."

"Mac, that's the way parish priests have operated since the church opened its doors for business." Terry smiled.

"A little test, my community spiritual leader. Wyvonny's a murderer. Did you know that?"

"She killed the old man with a big kitchen knife, didn't she?" He managed to keep a straight face.

"Lily Dell's really a world-class gossip, isn't she?"

"When's the wedding?" he asked. "It'll have to be put off a few weeks now, I suppose. Only proper, considering."

"What wedding!" I shouted. "We're talking funerals."

"Forget it. Maybe I spoke out of turn," he said.

"Terry, give me a break."

"Mrs. Binford's. She's getting married again, according to Lily Dell. Who got it, of course, from Wyvonny."

"Who? This is all news to me."

"Some publisher, or former publisher, I guess it is. From North Carolina, as I recall. He got pushed out of his job by a buyout, I gather. He's supposed to be a very capable fellow," Terry said. He was enjoying this.

"When? Did Lily Dell confess that to you?"

"This is not confession. She just likes to talk. And no, she didn't. Mrs. Binford didn't mention this to you?"

"No, not a word," I said. And as far as I knew, not to anybody else, not to her stepchildren, not to Joab Wolfe. Only to Wyvonny, who had told Lily Dell, who had told Terry Riley. Who had told me.

"A singular family," he said. "Who should I contact about the memorial service?"

"I guess me. I don't think any of them really care so long as words are said. I think it's all for the children. Peter Stallings never would have won a popularity contest in that house, believe me."

"What about the body?" he asked.

"Noah Simmons has released it. Cremation, then burial in a small town in North Florida. There'll be no body at the house, if that's got you worried."

"No, no, I'm not worried about anything. I'll do the service, of course." He slapped me on my shoulder. "I look on it as missionary work."

12

IT'S EXACTLY LIKE an Alfred Hitchcock movie set, isn't it?" Polly Binford Theobald said in a loud whisper, and she was not far off the mark.

Peter Stallings's memorial service was held, at his wife's request, on the pondside gazebo at high noon on a gloomy, foggy day that spewed an occasional spurt of chilly rain like a near-empty seltzer-water bottle. Some thoughtful person had arranged vases of cut flowers from the garden, placed them randomly around on the treated pine floor, as if no one had thought to do so until the very last minute.

All the women were properly dressed in black. I wore a blue suit, an old Marshall Field bargain-basement special, Joab Wolfe dark and proper gray, and off-the-wall Freeport Junior blue seersucker. Cyril Theobald wore black wheat jeans and a black T-shirt. Father Terrance Riley wore a black toes-length cassock that covered his leg cast, and Lily Dell, Wyvonny, and Lincoln were dressed in their gray-black uniforms.

I don't know what I expected Lily Dell to look like. Mammy in *Gone With the Wind,* something like that, I suppose. She didn't, of course. She was stout, not fat, and solemn-faced that morning. But, surprisingly, hers was a face without defining character. I had expected more, but Lily Dell looked like an ordinary sixty-year-old black woman you see on the streets of Chicago dozens of times every day.

Terry Riley took a firm neutral middle ground in his conduct of the services. He read the appropriate Scriptures and concluded with a passage from one of John Donne's sermons on the democracy of death:

"The ashes of an oak in the chimney are no epitaph of that oak to tell me how high or large that was; it tells me not what flocks it sheltered, while it stood, nor what men it hurt when it fell. . . ."

Bitsy nodded her head in solemn agreement. Sally Ann bit her lip. "Good thing, too," Polly murmured, meaning for it to be overheard.

Joab and Freeport Junior then took turns reading messages of condolence sent by various company executives, a newspaper editor in Cordele, Georgia, a television-station manager in High Point, North Carolina, a publisher in Aiken, South Carolina, others, and by various elected officials, mayors, state representatives, three different governors. Without exception, their words, written, of course, by their press secretaries, expressed shock over the untimely death of Freeport Communications' chief executive and praised his daring and vision.

Sally Ann, dressed in starched and shining black cotton, stood with her arms around her two children. The three of them cried softly, but nobody else did.

And that was it. The whole thing took about fifteen minutes. Then Bloody Marys and light snacks were served on the back porch. And so much for the youthful executive. After the service not a word was said about him.

After a suitable interval, the children were led away by Wyvonny and Lily Dell for cable-television cartoons and naps. Freeport Junior, gosh darn it, had some personal "bidness" in town he simply had to take care of. Golf, if it doesn't rain, at Westward Ho, Polly whispered loudly. Cyril disappeared, and a few minutes later I spotted him jogging through the estate's pine trees, bearing two rather hefty dumbbells in his hands, pumping them as he ran, and darting through the pine trees like a Cape deer spooked by a rifle shot.

Southern women of a certain age and usually not of the immediate family try to be upbeat at wakes. They bring cakes and fried chicken. They hurry about, paying attention to the smallest request or overlooked detail. They speak in whispers, but otherwise pretend to ignore the reason for the gathering. They provide a certain continuity, a sense that life does indeed go on.

Driven perhaps by her intuition, Bitsy attempted to play that role on the porch that afternoon, except she didn't whisper.

"Father Riley, it is so good of you to help us out. Especially in your condition, you poor man. I'll certainly be making a contribution," she said to Terry. "Mac, do have another of those crabmeat things Lily Dell has made.

You're such a dear old thing to help me get through this," she said to me. "Polly, you're definitely losing weight," she told her oldest stepdaughter, who was indiscriminately devouring hors d'oeuvres. And, "Weren't the children lovely? Such brave little soldiers," she said to Sally Ann. "You must get some rest, dear."

As so many new widows try to be, Sally Ann was very with-it, bright-eyed, and under intense self-control. And never without a fresh Bloody Mary in her hands. Her pupils were dilated and the smile was plastered on her mouth, and I wondered what trank she was on.

Terry Riley obviously was anxious to resume his surveillance of his parish school's restoration. He had visions of new commodes and sturdy oak flooring in his mind. When he said his proper good-byes and I moved to help him hobble out to my old car, Sally Ann suddenly insisted that she go along with us for the ride, and who was to say no to the widow du jour? So she piled in with us.

"Thank you, thank you. I just need to get away from that whole thing for a few minutes," she said when we were under way. And after we dropped Terry off at the rectory, she said, "I can't bear to go back to that house quite yet. Take me someplace for a rainy-afternoon drink."

It wasn't raining, but thence—where else?—to the Binnacle we repaired, where workmen on stepladders were hanging a new sign over the entrance. FOOD FOR THE HUNGRY, DRINK FOR THE THIRSTY, it proclaimed.

"I personally like it. It's got class and originality," I told Nickey when we were seated at the bar. "Especially I like the Old English lettering."

"Yeah, I ordered it before I sold the joint, and I paid Nina in advance to make it. So I figured," he said with a shrug.

"Maybe a vodka on the rocks," Sally Ann said. "Make it Stoli."

Nickey looked at me, raised one eyebrow.

"And for me, coffee. Hot coffee. My usual," I cried.

The drinks were served. My coffee was in a beer mug big enough to float an ox in. I think if I'd tried to order alcohol from Nickey at that moment he would have slugged me.

Sally Ann sipped her vodka. "I certainly hope you don't think I'm trying to flirt with you," she said.

"I certainly don't," I said.

"Because I don't intend to be any merry widow or anything such as that."

Nickey watched while I poured cream in my coffee.

"I mean, inviting myself to take a drive with you might give a person the wrong idea," Sally Ann said.

"I didn't get any wrong idea," I said. "I took you at your word when you said you wanted a break, that's all."

"Of course, Peter and I did have a very active sex life together. I won't deny that. And I don't intend to spend the rest of my life alone. But not quite yet, thank you very much all the same," she said.

"Of course," I said. "I don't think anybody expects you to do that."

"When I say a very active sex life, I mean extremely active, if you get what I mean."

"I see." I glanced at Nickey, who was taking it all in, of course. He rolled his eyes up to the ceiling.

"Morning, noon, and night," she said. "The honeymoon never ended in that regard." She finished her vodka and signaled Nickey for another one. He glanced at me. I shrugged. He poured.

"I'm separated from my wife," I said. "What I mean is, I know what it feels like to be alone."

"What am I going to do with myself? Is that what you're asking? I'm really not sure yet. Maybe I'll leave Freeport. Move to Atlanta, maybe. That's a nice town."

"Everybody seems to like it."

"Or I've thought about going back to school. To study psychiatry. Or psychology, I mean. I've always been interested in the human brain. And what makes it tick."

"That's certainly a big subject," I said. "That could keep a person busy a long time."

"Or maybe I'll travel. A long trip. Around the world. Leave the children with Mother Bitsy and Wyvonny. Mother Bitsy suggested that, as a matter of fact. She said cost would be no object. Gay Paree, ooh la la."

"They have some very good tours," I said. "I guess we ought to think about getting back."

"Why? You think they think we're out in the bushes or something?"

"Of course not."

She finished her second vodka with a big gulp and slid the glass across the bar to Nickey. "One more and that's it for this little girl," she said.

"And I'll have another brimming, steaming mugful of that delicious coffee," I said. "No vodka for me, thanks."

"Well, anyhoo, as I was saying, the idea of any sort of affair or sexual liaison is going to be a long time coming for this widow lady," Sally Ann said. "It's going to take me a long time to get Peter out of my mind."

"That's only natural."

"At first I thought somebody had killed him," she said. "I mean, Peter had more than his share of enemies. But the more I thought about it, the more I could see how he would . . . do what he did. What do you think the last thought in his brain was? Before the lights went out for keeps, I mean?"

"Maybe a single vodka on the rocks for me," I said. Nickey made no move.

"That sounds very morbid, I realize. And I'm truly sorry," Sally Ann said.

"You've got to put thoughts like that out of your head," I said, wondering what her reaction would be if I had told her of my own suspicion concerning her husband's death.

"I'm sure I'll get remarried. Of course, not right away. But someday. I mean, I am still fairly young and I'm not *unattractive*. Do you think I'm attractive, Mac? No, don't answer that, please. There I go, sounding like I'm flirting again when my husband's not even buried yet."

"No, under the circumstances you sound fine. And, yes, Sally Ann, you're attractive."

"May I ask you a very intimate question?"

"I suppose."

"Let's say you and I don't know each other, we meet, and you're attracted to me. You ask me, Sally Ann, are you divorced, or what? I answer, No, my husband blew his brains out. What would your reaction be to that?"

"Well . . ."

"Would you still think I was attractive?"

"We've really got to be getting back, Sally Ann," I said.

"One more drink. I really need one more to get through this. I almost never drink, did you know that? One more, and then you can take me home and put me to bed. I don't mean actually put me to bed. Don't go getting any ideas. You can deliver me."

"You can have one more at home," I said. I settled up with Nickey.

"I'll let you know one thing," she said. "I intend to keep the memory of their father alive in the brains of my two children. That's a vow I've taken to myself."

"Come on," I said, helping her rise from her barstool. "A little nap wouldn't hurt you."

"Are you making a pass at me? Was that a pass? What did you mean by a little nap?"

Nickey rolled his eyes up to the ceiling again.

13

BY THE TIME I got back to Belle Haven, Sally Ann was asleep, her head back on the seat, mouth open, snoring with wild abandon. I had been there myself once or twice, so I decided to let her snooze it off in the car. I parked just outside the garage of the addition, in the shade, slipped out of the car, and walked through the front door of the main house. Wyvonny was waiting in the center hallway, a warning finger held to her lips.

"I seen you drive up. Don't you go out there," she whispered urgently. "Just between the two of them, and a long time coming. None of your business."

I could hear voices, angry, embittered voices.

"It's Miss Bitsy and that Polly. I ain't never seen Miss Bitsy so mad," Wyvonny whispered.

The house was open, all windows raised and all doors agape, blocked back by bricks covered with a teenage Sally Ann's needlepoint *(Summer 1969. Belle Haven. First Man on Moon. SAB)* and, by listening closely, I could easily hear the two women's voices. Wyvonny was right. It was a classic mother-daughter alleycat fight.

"You don't give one good damn about the company, do you?" I heard Bitsy say. "You only care about its worth. To you."

"I'm interested in what's mine. Is there anything immoral about that?" Polly replied.

"Most of what you refer to as yours I made for you," Bitsy said. "If all you stood to come by was what your father initially left you, it wouldn't come to very much, I assure you. Not enough to keep you and your husband for a year."

"You really are a miser, aren't you? You want to keep it all to yourself. Ration it out to us in bits and dabs."

"Well, that is why you want us to sell the company, isn't it? To support your fourth husband's, pardon me if I smile, artistic output?"

"You're not my real mother. I've always been well aware of that. I've never really thought of you that way. But until now I did think of you as a friendly presence."

"This be real heavy shit," Wyvonny whispered to me. "I ain't never heard the two of them talk to each other like this before." She and I were standing in the hallway like two statues in Madame Tussaud's wax museum. Out of there, that was where I desperately wanted to be. Such eavesdropping by Wyvonny might be understandable. But not by me. I felt like a common snoop. Yet I couldn't move.

"Polly, I'm sorry to say it, but my feelings about you

1 4 5

also are becoming more and more ambivalent," Bitsy said.

"I'm sorry it's come to this. But I'm as stubborn as you are, Mother Bitsy. You should know. I've talked to a lawyer."

"A lawyer!" Bitsy exclaimed, as if her stepdaughter had been consulting with some witch doctor who examined chicken entrails to foresee their future. "And what, pray tell, did this fancy New York *lawyer* tell you, Polly?"

"He told me that I've got a case if you don't offer me a fair price for my share of the stock."

"Indeed! I had no idea you and your fourth husband were so financially desperate, my dear Polly."

"Nobody likes being cut out of things," Polly said.

"What *things*? We don't publish *The New York Review of Books*. We publish small-town newspapers. Nothing you and your Number Four would be interested in, I assure you."

"Please stop referring to Cyril by the numbers."

"However many. I lose count, Polly. But the fact remains, somebody had to stay home and do the dirty work, wash the dishes, take out the garbage, while you went up North and played."

"Look, I'm sorry Peter didn't work out for you," Polly said. "But a fact's a fact. He went loco on you. All the more reason you should come to your senses and sell. You're too old to start over, Mother Bitsy."

"Well, I never," Bitsy said. "Such vehemence, such viciousness, while speaking of your sister's husband. Could it be because you and Peter had such a horrible argument down at the gazebo the day before he died?"

There was a long pause in the dialogue. I could imagine the two of them standing there, staring at each other. Finally Polly said softly, "You amaze me. Truly."

"He slapped your face for you, didn't he?" Bitsy cried. "I understand you were staggered backward by the blow."

"Lincoln saw us. It must have been," Polly said to herself. "Who told Lily Dell, who told Wyvonny, who told you, of course."

"And now I know why it happened, of course," Bitsy said. "Peter learned you were shopping the company around behind our backs, confronted you with that fact, and slapped your face for you when you fessed up. I don't blame him. Because I feel like doing the same thing myself."

"Try it and you'll get slapped right back," Polly said.

Bitsy gasped. After collecting herself, she said quietly and evenly, "You and your husband are no longer welcome at Belle Haven. I want the two of you out as soon as possible."

"You can kick me out of the house, but not out of the company. You remember that. You're going to have to deal with me sooner or later." I could hear Polly's heavy footsteps as she walked purposefully down the backstairs and off the porch. Going to find her running, sweating fourth husband? Perhaps.

"Wyvonny!" Bitsy was ringing her crystal bell as if the back porch were on fire.

"Coming this very second, Miss Bitsy!" Wyvonny cried. She hurried out the screened door.

"I desperately need something strong. Hot coffee perhaps. Without cream."

I was tempted to sneak up to my room for a while, but I decided I couldn't do that. Bitsy was my friend, and I had accepted her hospitality with the understanding that I would try to be of help to her during a trying time, and this surely seemed like one of those to me. I regretted the fact that I also was a messenger bearing more bad news, but there was nothing I could do about that.

"Make it two, Wyvonny," I said, and walked out on the porch feeling like a kid reporter with a lead that hadn't worked out.

The rain had passed out to sea, the sun was out, and the air smelled clean and grassy. Lincoln must have mowed earlier that morning. Clam Pond was busy, at its summer's glory. At the far end the small beach was crowded, kids dripping sand, mothers dripping fat asses, young lifeguards of both sexes, muscles, curves, and action. Speedboats were towing water-skiers in fat circles. People were glorying in the sun, the suddenly cloudless sky, the beginning of afternoon of a perfect Cape Cod day. Why did it depress me so?

"Goodness me, Mac. I never!" Bitsy exclaimed. She looked very old, standing there on the porch, her thin arms clasped around her chest. "Did you hear all of that?"

"Polly told me last night at dinner that she was going to try to convince you to sell out. Obviously she means it," I said.

She sighed. "Those children. Have you ever? Even Sally Ann. They're all supposed to be grown. You and I were grown at their age. Remember? We thought like adults."

"So there's only you and Joab," I said.

She walked over to the railing of the porch. "There's

only me. Joab's as much a child as the rest of them when you get right down to it. I'm the only adult. The only one. The only one who does what must be done, I'm afraid."

I sat down in the glider. "Maybe your new husband will be a grown guy."

She turned. My words had startled her. "What? How did you know about that?"

"It doesn't matter," I said. "You probably do need somebody. Polly thought you were going to try to hire me."

She waved her hand in dismissal, as if the thought had never entered her mind. What an absurd idea, her wave said. I didn't say anything, but that didn't especially serve as a morale-booster. "To tell the truth, I thought it was a pretty absurd notion myself," I said.

"Look, even the children don't know about this yet," she said. "You aren't to say one word to anyone."

"What about Joab? I think he will be more than just a little interested."

She tried to laugh but found it difficult. "Joab'll see it as another threat to his job. Which, of course, it isn't. I've told you, Joab's simply another big baby, underneath all that bluster."

"I think it's time you and I had a talk, Bitsy," I said.

She recognized my false pomposity for what it was, but didn't challenge me, as once she would have done. Instead she rather meekly sat down in her favored wicker chair beside me and waited for me to speak, in the Southern way. Wyvonny came out and served the coffee. I waited until she had left us.

"Okay. I think somebody killed Peter Stallings," I said. "I don't think it was suicide. I think it was murder."

She wrapped her arms around herself again.

"Did you hear what I said?" I asked.

"I never. You give me the absolute shivers talking like that, Mac. You're talking about murder in my own family, right here in Belle Haven. I won't hear of it."

"I'm sorry, Bitsy. But you and I are adults, right?"

She reached over and touched my hand. "It's that old investigative reporter coming out in you, Mac."

"Peter was murdered. I know you've had to face a lot of things these past few days. Now you've got to face this, too."

"I'm not sure I can, with all its implications," she said. "Goodness, there is a limit, after all."

I took her thin hand in mine. "I don't like to say this. But you and I have always told each other the truth."

"Then tell me. Some intruder? Tell me that's the case."

I hesitated. "I wish I could," I said at last. "But I really don't think so."

"One of us? Here at Belle Haven? Is that what you're suggesting? I never! Murder at Belle Haven!"

"I'm sorry, Bitsy," I said with sincerity. "I know what that does to things."

She sipped her coffee. "What brings you to such a conclusion, Mac?" she asked. "You certainly have detected quite a lot that nobody else has. The police, for example. Chief Simmons has released Peter's body for burial, you know."

"The body had already been embalmed. Since then a lot of little things have added up."

"My. You sound like Monsieur Hercule Poirot. A lot of little things. Which have added up."

"Peter Stallings had a stroke. He hid it from you. From his wife, too, I think."

"Sally Ann certainly never mentioned anything like that to me," she said, her eyes widening. "A stroke? I never. He was so young. Surely you're wrong there."

"I'm told lots of people try to hide the fact that they've had a minor stroke. Bitsy, I talked with Dr. Cody down in Freeport. Peter went to see him secretly. And Cody's pretty sure Peter had a stroke."

"I see." She stared into her coffee cup. "But exactly what does that prove? Nothing that I can see."

I explained to her how a stroke could have affected the use of her son-in-law's right hand, and I told her about my own experience and how that had led me to my conclusion. "It also could help explain the man's erratic behavior," I said.

"I never noticed it," Bitsy said. "How stupid of me."

"Freeport Junior noticed it when they sailed that boat up here. He didn't know what it was, but he noticed it."

Bitsy sighed. "And I still don't understand what it is you're driving at. I'm sorry, but I don't."

"You found the revolver lying beside his right hand, remember? I don't think he had the strength in his right index finger to have pulled the trigger, Bitsy."

"Desperate people are capable of doing all sorts of things. Surely, Mac."

"Yes, I can understand that. But a man determined to kill himself wouldn't want to botch it, would he?" I asked.

She thought about it at length. "I suppose not. But Peter was not himself. He wasn't thinking logically."

"No, there are so many other things, things I won't go

into. Murder is the only way it adds up," I said. "I'm sorry."

She poured more coffee for both of us. She smiled. She leaned back in her chair and sipped her coffee. "Well then, have you decided which of us is the guilty party?"

"Come on, Bitsy."

"No. I'm interested. And it's your case to solve, Mac, after all." She gave me a little slap on my knee, an old habit she had.

"I don't know. I suppose each of you had a motive, in a way. I'm not the law. Hell, I'm unemployed." I tried to smile. "Maybe that's my problem. I've got too much free time to think."

"Well, let's try to solve it together, shall we? Remember how we used to sit in the city room and figure things out on stories, until we both decided it had to have happened a certain way?"

"Of course I remember."

"Usually we were right, too."

I didn't say anything. I knew I was dealing with a very intelligent woman. But now I suddenly realized I was dealing with somebody I really didn't know anymore. You see somebody, familiar face, familiar voice, lots of old memories in common, and you can forget how people can change over the years, become different people, really.

"Let's take Polly first, shall we?" Bitsy suggested. "You heard us talking out here. She and Peter argued violently, and he slapped her face for her. They never really got along from day one. And Polly desperately wants to sell the company, which is the last thing Peter wanted to do. Certainly a suspect, wouldn't you say?"

"Bitsy, I don't want to play this game with you," I said.

She continued as if I hadn't spoken. "And then there's Cyril. Such a common person. Polly married far beneath herself with that one, I don't mind telling you. And he has a rather violent background. Drugs. Arrests. A back-alley life until Polly came along and picked him up and dusted him off. Peter had nothing but contempt for him, and let Cyril know it every chance he had. And that little Number Four, Polly's fourth husband, I mean, walks around with a huge chip on his shoulder."

"I discovered that for myself."

"He also is totally dependent on Polly. Without her he'd starve," Bitsy said. "I can't abide him myself."

"Bitsy, I never said I was prepared to solve any crime," I told her. "I only said I think one has been committed."

"Freeport Junior, you get right down to it, wants the company to stake him to twenty-five million dollars or so to clear up his latest debts. He's a most desperate young man these days, you know." She took a deep breath and shook her head sadly. "And desperation can provoke all sorts of ugly, emotional responses. Freeport Junior may have determined that for him to have any chance at all of wheedling the money out of me, Peter would have to be, how do they say it, eliminated. Perhaps my stepson eliminated my son-in-law, Mac. What do you think?"

I knew she was playing games with me, so I decided to join right in. "Freeport Junior," I mused. "You know, I really hadn't thought of him. But I guess it's possible. A man in big debt. Yes, I can see it." I paused. "But I was thinking more about Joab Wolfe."

"Yes, you're right," Bitsy said immediately. "Peter got

him drunk and tried to get rid of him. A clumsy attempt, which never would have worked out. I'll always be protective of Joab, and Peter knew it. I still can't understand that one. But Peter always was a burr under Joab's saddle. No respect on either side. I'll have to think about that."

"And there's Wyvonny," I said. "A convicted murderer."

"Mac, may I tell you something? Wyvonny would kill the president of the United States if she got it in her mind I didn't approve of his foreign policy, for goodness sake!"

"Joab told me about the sexual advances Peter made," I said.

We sat there, drank our coffee, and looked at each other. "And last but not least there's little old me," Bitsy said with a smile. "Your old would-be, might-have-been sweetheart."

"Yes, I guess that's right," I said. This was what police homicide detectives were supposed to do. I was way over my head.

"That's really what you've thought all along, isn't it, Mac?" she asked. "Be honest with me now."

"Christ, Bitsy."

"That Bitsy Zimmerman, your old flame, has committed murder most foul?" She held up her hands in mock surrender. "Very well, you got me, coppers. I confess. I killed Peter Stallings."

"It's not funny, Bitsy," I managed to say.

She stood and paced about the porch. "God, what a fine afternoon. You never know what's going to happen to a summer's day here on the Cape, do you? Foggy and cloudy in the morning, raining, and it can keep on that way or clear up like this. Play it as it lays. Isn't that the smart expression, Mac?"

"It's my first summer here," I said.

She walked over and glared down at me. "Don't you want to hear the whys and how of it?" she demanded. "All the gruesome details? You're an old police reporter, Mac. You should be more than accustomed to gruesome details."

"Look, I'm not a cop and I'm not a priest. I'm not even a real newspaper reporter anymore."

"God, such an absolute mess," Bitsy moaned. She sat beside me on the glider and took my arm in hers, the way some people will when they want to share a confidence with an old friend. "Oh, Mac, he was *so* damned awful," she said.

"I don't doubt that, not for a minute," I said.

"What that crazy, absolutely insane young man put me through, with Sally Ann, with the company, with Joab. Well, you'll never know."

"Bits, you sound like you're complaining about our old managing editor," I said.

"I never. Nobody's called me Bits for years and years. It makes me feel absolutely young again," she said. She gave my arm a squeeze.

"If you really did it, I'm sure it wasn't premeditated," I said, seeing for a moment, I suppose, the young Bitsy in the old Bitsy. Such a black-haired beauty she had been.

"The answer to that, *of course*, is heavens no!" she cried. "You of all people know me better than that, Mac."

"Then exactly how did it happen?"

"I knew Joab was going down to that damned boat to

talk with Peter after dinner," she said after a moment's thought. "Joab didn't tell me. I could just feel it, knowing them both so well. So I sat here on the porch and waited, until I saw Joab struggling up the lawn, poor baby, staggering and cursing Peter for all he was worth."

"And after Joab went inside, you walked down to the boat to confront Peter?" I asked. "I can understand that. You'd had it."

"I truly don't know what I went down there to do. Have it out with him once and for all, I suppose. Fire him if necessary. I knew it couldn't go on any longer. Peter was wrecking everything I had worked so hard to build. The company, the family, Joab. I do know I was mad as a wet hen. You do know that expression, don't you, Mac?"

"It's made its way north," I said.

She touched my cheek. "You damn Yankees. You're all alike. You know I never really felt at home up there in Chicago. It was as if I'd been transferred to Russia or something. Maybe that's really why I married Freeport. To get out of there. I didn't love him. Half in love with you, I suppose, and knew you were way too young for me."

Did she know how old and thin and drawn she had become? Did she know how much I yearned for violet-eyed Kate? Did she know she was a stranger? "In any event, you went down to the boat determined to have a showdown with Peter," I said.

"Now don't you try to draw me out," she said. "Here I am telling you everything, and you're trying to draw me out."

Too much. "Bitsy, for God's sake, we're talking about

1 5 6

taking another human being's life!" I shouted. "In this case, your son-in-law's. He was somebody to you. Not exactly a stranger. Crazy or not, Peter Stallings was a member of your family. You don't just, bang, kill somebody like that."

"You don't. I know you don't. Of course you don't. My goodness, Mac. I never!"

"Okay. Okay. Okay," I said. "Just so we know this is serious business."

"Don't you think I know it's serious business?"

"Just tell me what happened?"

"I went aboard that boat. I called out. There was no answer. So I went down into the cabin. And I found Peter passed out, lolling on the couch. Snoring. With brandy on his breath and with his pistol on the table." She paused. "So I did it."

"You *did* it!" I shouted. "Just like that? Killed him? Said to yourself, I think I'll blow the bastard's brains out? And picked up the gun and did it? Give me a break."

"I know it sounds insane," Bitsy said. "No jury would ever believe me, right?"

"I didn't say that."

"But it's true. And what's more, it seemed to make perfect sense to me at the time. Temporary insanity, I suppose. I know I put the gun in his mouth, wrapped his finger around the trigger. And pulled it."

"The wrong finger of the wrong hand," I said.

"So it now appears."

"You invited me over for coffee the next morning. You knew full well there was a dead man lying on that boat

157

when we were sitting here talking about old times," I said. "You set me up, Bitsy."

She patted my hand. "I will admit I was playing a little trick on you."

"A little trick? Is that what you call it down in Georgia? You were making me part of the suicide cover-up. That pisses me off considerably, Bitsy. I don't mind telling you that."

"I took advantage of you. I know that." She placed a hand on my cheek. I felt as if she were grooming me. "But isn't that what old friends are for?"

"I always thought it was just the opposite." I paused. We both sat and thought for a moment, considering, I suppose, what we were drifting into, an ever-narrowing stream of less and less depth. Soon to hit rock bottom. "It did solve a lot of your problems for you, didn't it?" I said. "Doing Peter."

"What a gentle and most civilized way to describe it!"-she cried. "And the answer is yes, yes, and another yes. Yes."

"Weren't you horrified by what you'd done? The Bitsy Zimmerman I once knew would have been."

"I've not become inhuman, Mac," she said. "At first, of course I was. I pulled that trigger and got out of there. And I never laid eyes on the likes of him again. I couldn't bear to do that. But I do confess, the more I thought about it, as a little time passed, the better I felt about it."

Another silence between us.

"Well, better is not the word. Not at all. Relieved. I had such an utter sense of relief, with him gone."

"Bitsy, you executed him," I said.

She thought about that for a moment. "I suppose I did."

"And what do you plan to do next? I'm rather interested."

"Why, nothing. What do you expect?" she asked, her eyes widening.

"I may be wrong about this, but I think if I don't report this conversation to the police, it makes me an accessory after the fact," I said.

"Then you go right ahead," she said. "We certainly do not want you to become any accessory after any fact, do we? The very idea!"

"And what would you do then?"

"Why, deny every word of it, of course."

I threw up hands up in desperation. "I cannot believe you and I are having this conversation."

"Do you honestly think I would ever, ever confess to the authorities? I'm not that crazy, Mac," she said.

"Then why did you tell me?"

She waved her hand at me in dismissal in the old familiar way she had. "I needed to talk to somebody. That's a fairly heavy load to carry around, you know. I felt somebody had to know, somebody had to be told."

"Well, the autopsy was botched. That's in your favor," I said.

"Dear Mac. It's going to be all right. Really. It is. Except that you're such an old friend, there's really no reason for you to be concerned."

"Scarlett O'Hara. You sound more like her than you usually do."

159

She thought about that for a moment. "I suppose. In a way. A Southern woman trying to survive, trying to preserve what she's put together."

"I guess it is romantic to think of yourself that way," I said. "But what if it comes down to a murder investigation?"

"Would I confess and save everybody a lot of trouble? Is that what you're asking?"

"Yes."

"I've confessed to you, haven't I?" She gave me a firm pat on my knee. "That is quite enough confession for a while, thank you."

14

AS I RECALL, the word you used was *guaranteed*," I said to Noah Simmons. "That was the operative word, wasn't it?"

"So it was. But you must try and show a little patience," he said. "Have you never been fishing before? Do you recall President Bush's experience in these same waters? He went for days before his patience was rewarded. With a nice nine-pounder, as I remember."

"I am being patient," I said. "I've been patient for nearly three hours now."

We were aboard the *Nolo Contendee*, a twenty-four-foot motor cruiser that was the pride and newest possession of the lawyer Bascombe Midgeley, given to him in lieu of payment for services rendered by a grateful client who, according to Bascombe, had walked out of a bitter divorce settlement dead broke but freed from future alimony payment.

We were in Nantucket Sound, about two miles out of the Cut, the break in Cape Cod's eastern shoreline that allows the waters of the sound to flow into and constantly refresh North Walpole's Pilgrim Harbor. It was eight in the morning, we had been fishing since sunrise, and so far the ice locker was still empty.

It was a gray and chilly morning, and Bascombe was wearing an olive-colored oilskin jacket, buttoned to its neck, and he had Band-Aids plastered all over his face. Rocko Murphy, a true street fighter, bit, gouged, and scratched as well as hit and kicked.

Bascombe normally received clients in his oak-paneled law office dressed in dark three-piece suits, silk bow ties, and Church's shoes, a very proper figure of a Harvard Law man, a bit overweight and much too pompous for his own good. But all Cape Cod natives seem at home on salt water. You see little old ladies out tooling around in cat-boats, for God's sake. And on his boat, Bascombe was like a kid on a new bike.

This was an excursion the three of us had been planning for weeks, and I had slipped out of Belle Haven before first light that morning to be on time for it.

I should have told Noah about Bitsy Binford's confession the second I laid eyes on him, before we left the fishing dock, but I didn't. I had left Belle Haven determined to do exactly that, but I didn't. It was a beautiful morning, and I was lonely and in need of some of that male bonding, so I decided my news could wait a couple of hours. Bitsy wasn't going anywhere. And, boy, was I wrong about that.

"Wait a minute!" I cried. "I think I've caught a whale."

"Let me have a feel." Noah took the rod from my

hands, and I didn't protest. He reeled in a few feet, heavy going for him, too, he whose strength is as the strength of ten, make it a dozen.

"Pot?" Bascombe asked.

"Feels like it," Noah said.

"Tell this landlubber all about it," I said.

"Probably a lobster pot," Bascombe said. "It's not all that unusual for summer people to go to city hall, pay fifteen dollars for a license and put out a pot, then check it whenever they sail out here. Gives the kids a little something different to do on vacation. Except the commercial lobstermen cut their buoys because they don't want any amateur competition. There're only so many lobsters, after all."

"How do they know the difference?" I asked.

"Every guy who lobsters out here for a living . . . has his own . . . special buoy markings," said Noah, huffing and puffing and reeling away. "Like a ranch has . . . a brand for its cattle. You honor them."

"I'd offer to help you, take turns. But you're the son of a fisherman, and I can tell you're enjoying this," I said.

"Here," he said, handing me the rod. "Your turn to have fun."

It took the three of us, taking turns reeling in, the better part of fifteen minutes to bring it up, a raw, water-soaked wooden cage dripping weed, and haul it on board the boat. And the damn thing was empty.

"Noah, off my port bow," Bascombe said sharply.

Noah shaded his eyes with the palm of his hand and looked in the direction Bascombe was pointing. The surface there, a hundred yards or so ahead of us, was rippling and busy, the water churning, although I hadn't noticed it. Bascombe headed in that direction.

"Blues feeding," Noah said. "*Pomatomus saltatrix.* Just like I guaranteed." A policeman by profession, a marine biologist by university training, and a Latin freak by inclination, Noah often lapsed into what he called his stepmother tongue among friends.

We trolled through the feeding ground, and we had not gone far before Noah's rod bent and the line went taut. He reeled in furiously, setting the hook, and seconds later the big bluefish came out of the water, bending and thrashing, trying to shake the hook, blue-green and silverbellied against the gray sky of the morning.

"You got at least fifteen pounds there, and he's mad as hell!" Bascombe shouted.

A second fish hit my line then, the force of the strike almost pulling my rod from my hands, and, seconds later, Bascombe's was taken. "We've run into a big school of them!" Noah shouted happily.

I had never fished for blues before, and I was surprised both by their strength and anger. They simply do not like being caught, and they don't give up without a fight, much more fight per pound than any other light-tackle fish I had ever known. With a big one, make that medium-sized, you got your hands full. Soon we had three taut lines crisscrossing behind Bascombe's boat as the fish maneuvered to free themselves.

"Careful now, let's don't get our lines tangled," Noah said. "Don't try to move around. Hand the rods back and forth, right after the lines cross in the water."

That is how we handled it. We were using hooked silver spoons and phosphorescent orange-colored surgical tubing for bait. Between us we landed eleven of them, and by the time we had netted them and pulled them on board, my shirt was soaked with sweat and my back was beginning to ache.

Noah wore leather gloves and used pliers to extract the hooks, and he worked with great care and caution when he flipped them into the ice locker, because blues have a mouth filled with jagged, razor-sharp teeth.

We fished for another hour, until the locker was filled and I was ready to check into the nearest rest home. Then they stopped biting as suddenly as they had begun. We trolled for another half hour or so without further luck. "A nice run," Noah said.

When our catch had stopped bumping and flapping in the ice locker, Noah took a long, thin knife from his tackle box, sharpened it on a grooved whetstone, and started filleting the fish expertly, using the locker top as a cutting table and tossing heads, bones, and entrails into the boat's wake for the gang of sea gulls that was following us.

He tossed the fillets into a bucket of seawater as he stripped them off the sides of the fish, and by the time he had finished, the afterdeck of the boat was bloody, and so were Noah's hands and arms, up to his elbows.

I grabbed another bucket, filled it from the boat's side, allowed Noah to wash his hands and arms in it, then sloshed several bucketfuls on the locker top and the deck, until they were clean.

"You're pretty good with that knife," I said.

"I ought to be. I used it enough when I was a kid. It was my dad's knife," Noah said.

"That's one good thing about you Cape Codders. You keep things," I said. "I didn't realize blues were such mean bastards."

"They'll bite your finger off it you're not careful. And they're too oily for most people's taste."

"One must broil them the very day they're caught, only hours later if possible. Then they are delicious. But never, never order them in a restaurant," Bascombe said. "They only run in these waters late, toward the end of the summer. They'll be heading south again very soon."

"I'll smoke these if you two agree," Noah said.

"Noah's got an old refrigerator with holes cut in the top to let the smoke out, Mac," Bascombe said. "He cuts the fillets into little pieces and lays them on the racks inside."

"Blues are the best smoked fish in the world," Noah said. "They lose all the oil in the smoking. It drips on the coals and flavors the fish."

Noah's expertise, Bascombe's boat, and my chow. I had brought cans of Narragansett beer, kept cold in the ice locker, and sandwiches made for me at Bob's Sandwich Shop with dill bread, homemade cream cheese, and thick slices of beefeater tomatoes. There was orange pound cake for dessert.

Bascombe headed the *Nolo Contendee* back toward the Cut. I figured it was as good a time as any.

"I've picked up a little information," I said to Noah.

"I've been wondering when you were going to get around to that."

I poured all of us black coffee into paper cups from a

Thermos. "Bitsy Binford told me she killed her son-in-law," I said.

Noah had finished his cake. There was one more sandwich in the paper bag, and he eyed it.

"Go ahead," I said. "I'll take it out in smoked fish."

He unwrapped the sandwich. "Did she go into particulars?"

"She said she went down to the boat after Joab Wolfe had left that night, found Peter Stallings passed out drunk on the couch, the gun on the table. She put it in his mouth, wrapped his finger around the trigger, and blew him away."

Noah was like a blue feeding. Half the sandwich was already gone. "Not exactly accidental," he managed to say.

"She didn't claim it was. She said she did it on impulse. She used the words 'temporary insanity.' "

He looked at me long and hard. "You thought she did it all along, didn't you?"

"Not at first," I said. "I didn't want it to be her. But things kept adding up. She's also argued with her oldest stepdaughter, who wants to sell out. She's announced to one and all that she's going to be running things again. And she's getting remarried. Some newspaper executive from North Carolina."

"She's been a busy lady."

"Noah, she told me if you ask her about it, she'll deny it. As far as she's concerned, it's suicide."

Bascombe had been listening intently. "Please inform Mrs. Binford I will be glad to take her case. Not guilty verdict guaranteed."

"What makes you so sure of that?" I asked him.

"I understand the body's been cremated, for one thing."

"Not yet," Noah said. "I've had the mortuary hold that up."

"But the body has been washed and embalmed," Bascombe said. "There's simply no evidence left to discover. You've got no proof that Mrs. Binford did anything. Except discover the body. Which she readily admits. Any lawyer could win that case."

"I'm afraid you're right," Noah said. "Not to mention the fact that I'm dealing with an important, established summer family here. *Nihil nimis.* It would cause an uproar in the community."

"*Good morning,* Mrs. Etheridge. Have a nice sail, Mr. Nickerson." Bascombe was waving and saying hello to friends and acquaintances who were on their way out of Pilgrim Harbor for a day in the Sound.

"Understand, I'm not giving up on this thing," Noah said. "But it's difficult. And it sure as hell puts you on the spot, Mac."

"Don't worry about that," I said. "I must say, you didn't seem surprised when I told you Bitsy confessed."

"If you conclude it wasn't suicide, it makes sense, I suppose."

"What are you going to do?"

"I'm going to have a talk with Bitsy Binford, first off."

"She's a smart cookie and a tough bird," I said. "If you think you'll rag her into confessing to you, you're wrong. I know her too well." I poured the rest of the coffee.

168

"You can't win them all, Noah," Bascombe said. "A hell of a lot of murderers go unpunished. You know that."

"And you think she will?" I asked.

"I sure do," Bascombe said.

"At least she'll know that I know," Noah said. "I'll make sure of that."

"It's not as if she's going to kill anybody else," I said. "The guy was driving her crazy. She just snapped."

"Chief Simmons, dispatcher."

Noah never set foot out of his office without his trusty Motorola. He pressed the "send" button and spoke into it. "Simmons here."

"Chief, we've just received a telephone call reporting an accidental death. Sounds like a drowning."

"Who? Where? How?"

"Belle Haven, that big yellow house out on Clam Pond," the dispatcher said. *"A Mrs. Binford. The cook called."*

15

CYRIL THEOBALD was sitting on the back-porch steps, dressed in sweat-stained running togs, his legs spread. He was pale of face and was gazing vacantly out at the waters of Clam Pond. His wife, Polly, was kneeling beside him with a hand on his shoulder. They were the first people Noah and I saw after we parked in the driveway at Belle Haven and ran around to the back of the house.

Polly looked up at us. "Cyril found her. He was out running," she said quietly.

"Where?" Noah asked urgently.

"He ran back to the house for help. Which was the right thing to do. I keep telling him that," she said. "Now he's just sitting here in a state of catatonic shock. He really did the right thing. I keep telling him that. Cyril's sensitive, an artist. Please tell him he did the right thing."

"Where's your mother!" I shouted.

She glared at us, a wild look in her eyes. "Can't you see? Damn you. Attention must be paid to my husband!" she

170

screamed furiously. "Do you hear me? Do you hear me? My husband needs medical and psychological attention immediately!"

I glanced at Noah, who threw both his hands in the air in disgust. Then, beyond him, sitting in Bitsy's wicker chair on the porch, I saw Wyvonny, as quiet as Cyril in her way. Noah and I ran up the porch steps to her.

"Wyvonny!" I cried.

"Miss Bitsy be dead," she said quietly. "Lily Dell be with her."

"But where, Wyvonny? Where?" I was shouting.

She pointed. "Out yonder. Down by the shore."

Beyond the borders of the lawn a thicket of pines burned by acid rain grew nearly to the pond's shore, replaced there by random silverleafs, a nuisance tree that springs up and spreads like weeds on Cape Cod shorelines.

Noah took off on the run, bounding down the porch steps and loping like a hungry grizzly across the lawn, and I followed him, huffing and puffing. A trail led through the woods alongside the pond shore, the trail Cyril Theobald must have followed on his morning run, and it was there, only a few yards down the trail, lying under the silverleaf trees, that we finally found Bitsy Binford's body. Lily Dell, who was standing there, keeping guard, had covered it with a sheet.

She didn't speak when we ran up.

Noah immediately jerked the sheet away. Bitsy was wearing a modest one-piece bathing suit and a white plastic bathing cap. I was a kid marine in Korea. Anybody who has ever seen dead people would know that Bitsy was dead. Noah knelt beside her to make an examination.

"She be dead," Lily Dell said to me. "Dead when that man of Polly's pulled her out of the water, I reckon. Shore mike was dead when I get here."

"No pulse," Noah said. "No life sign of any kind. Mac, I'm afraid she's had it."

I looked down at her frail white body. Somebody, perhaps death itself, had closed her eyes. My old flame. Little Bitsy. Death makes you think of people's younger days, doesn't it? I thought about our times together in Chicago, black-haired, beautiful Bitsy Zimmerman and young, ambitious, and amorous Mac, crime, swindle, and corruption solvers we were together. Also, one fine night I'd fucked her. Let us not forget that, I thought.

"What happened?" I asked Lily Dell.

"Used to be, Miss Bitsy'd slip down here most ever' morning, unless it be raining, she wouldn't bother then, hated to swim in that rain, sit on the porch and drink her coffee, and go swimming," the old woman said.

"I see. I remember she told me once she was on her college swimming team," I said.

Noah was still examining Bitsy's body, and taking his own good time about it. He was careful to keep his back to us so neither the old woman nor I could observe his actions.

"Shoot, that woman swim on her back, on her side, on her belly, any which a way," Lilly Dell said with pride in her voice.

"She was a fine swimmer," I said. So how did she drown?

" 'Course, getting on as she was, not as old as me, but

1 7 2

then ain't nobody as old as me, she cut way back on her swimming. Ever' now and then last summer, but near none this year." She looked down on Bitsy's body in sorrow. "Poor thing. Skinny as a sparrow, ain't she? No meat on her bones at all. Poor old thing. Seem like this summer the only time she come down here and go swimming be when she worried or couldn't get something off her mind. Tell me once, It relaxes me, Lily Dell, like nothing else in this world."

Noah turned to her. "Lily Dell, did you see her leave the house this morning?"

"Shore didn't. You can't see the pond from the kitchen."

"Well, somebody did," Noah muttered to himself.

"You through? Can I cover her again with this sheet?"

"Yes. Go ahead."

"Don't seem right, her laying there, so frail, with nothing over her." She spread the sheet over Bitsy's body. "No, she didn't," she said. "Didn't say anything about going swimming."

"I know how close you were to Mrs. Binford," Noah said.

"Treated me and Lincoln like we was members of her own family," she said.

"I think I know how bad you feel right now," he said.

Lily Dell didn't answer, but her lower lip trembled slightly. "I could use a dip of snuff," she said at last.

"I badly need to know what exactly happened here this morning, as you saw it," Noah said.

"I gets up early, first one ever' day," she said. "That Miss Bitsy there's usually second, and likes her coffee to be ready. Polly's fool husband out running his fool head off, too, usually by sunrise."

"Did you lay eyes on Miss Bitsy this morning, Lily Dell?" I asked.

"No, I didn't. I got up, made a fresh batch of biscuits, and put the coffee on. Usually by the time it's perked, Miss Bitsy, she be waiting for it on the back porch when I bring it out to her."

"But not this morning," Noah said.

"Coffee just starting to perk when that fool man of Polly's come tearing into the house, screaming his fool head off."

"Screaming because he'd come across Mrs. Binford's body while he was out running," Noah said.

"And that was about all I could get out of him that made any sense," Lily Dell said.

"Cyril's still pretty shook up," I said. "Polly's looking after him."

"Like always, that good-for-nothing," Lily Dell said. "Wouldn't even come back here with me. I had to walk down here and find Miss Bitsy by myself."

"You found the body here, where it is now?" Noah asked. Bitsy lay only a few feet away from the shoreline of the pond.

"He say he found her floating facedown in the water. Pull her out and come running for help back to the house. Screaming like a stuck pig. 'Course, I don't believe a word he say."

"Where is everybody?" I asked.

"Sally Ann out riding her children around, I don't know if she's told them yet. First they daddy, then they grand-

174

mama. Mr. Baby, he running around like a chicken with his head cut off.

"Where's Mr. Joab?" I asked.

"I reckon he be taking Miss Bitsy's passing real hard. He thought the world of that woman. Shore nuff did," Lily Dell said.

"I'm sure he did. But where is he?" Noah asked.

"Never come down here."

"So you don't know. And you don't know if he knows," Noah said. He turned to me. "Let's go back to the house. I've got to call Hamish Percival and get the rescue squad over here, which is starting to become a regular thing, the more I think of it."

"I be staying right here with Miss Bitsy," Lily Dell said. She took a small can of Bruton snuff from her apron pocket, together with a tiny, well-worn wooden paddle, dipped out a little heaping mound of the snuff, and packed it inside her bottom lip. She was still standing silently, looking down at Bitsy Binford's sheet-enshrouded body, as Noah and I walked away.

"So much for your murderer and her confession," he said as we walked out of the woods.

"It was a drowning accident, right?" I said. "That doesn't mean she didn't kill Peter Stallings," I protested.

"It was no drowning, Mac," Noah said urgently. "I didn't want to say anything in front of that old woman. But while you two were talking, I slipped Mrs. Binford's bathing cap off her head a little. Somebody bashed your old friend's brains out for her. The back of her head was all caved in."

"Murder," I said.

"Some bad person," he said.

We were just walking out of the pine thicket when we heard the sudden sharp crack of a pistol shot. We both turned toward the sound.

"Down there!" Noah cried. "It came from the *Comchi.*"

We ran down to the boat, and when we got there we found Freeport Junior lying facedown in the cockpit. He obviously had fallen flat on his belly the second the shot was fired.

"Freeport Junior," I whispered urgently. Noah drew his gun.

"Uncle Joab, don't blame yourself. That's all I'm trying to say," Freeport Junior called out.

"And I'm trying to tell you to get the hell off this boat and leave me the hell alone," Joab called back. He was in the cabin.

"Not until you come up out of there. No way."

Joab squeezed off another shot, and this time wood flew. Freeport Junior leapt off the boat, to the dock where Noah and I were standing. "Jesus Christ!" he cried. "First he says he was going to kill himself, and now he tries to kill me."

"You aren't worth the trouble," Joab called out. "But, yes, I will, if you show your ass on this boat again. Who's that out there with you, anyway?"

"Joab, it's me, McFarland," I said.

No answer.

"I know about Bitsy," I said.

"Not all you don't."

"Well, I know she's dead," I said. "Can I come on board?"

"Have Freeport Junior get away from this boat. Then

176

I'll think about it. Stupid shit never understands a damn thing, and I'm out of the explaining business."

"Okay." I motioned to Freeport Junior, waving him back.

"Mac, there's an armed man on that boat," Noah whispered. "And he sounds half-crazy to me. Don't be a damn fool. Let me handle this."

"Well, let the record show I damn well tried," Freeport Junior said. "Now I say let the damn fool kill himself if that's what he's determined to do."

"Let the record also show that I never liked you, you little turd," Joab called out. "Not even when you were a kid, and especially not now."

"He's leaving, Joab," I said. "You, too, Noah," I whispered. "Let me try to deal with him."

"Careful. Remember, you don't know what you've got on your hands here," he whispered back. He turned to leave, then thought better of it. "Mr. Wolfe, Police Chief Simmons here," he said in a loud, commanding voice.

"Ah, the plot thickens. You're coming in loud and clear, Chief."

"Then hear this. Mac here seems determined to talk to you. I want you to know he's doing it against my best advice. I also want you to know I won't be far away." He and I looked at each other. "I also want you to know he's a personal friend of mine, and if anything happens to him, I'll come back down here and kill you. You understand that?" He took Freeport Junior by his arm and led him up the lawn, twenty or thirty yards away.

"They're gone," I said to Joab.

"Then welcome aboard," he replied.

I climbed aboard *Comchi* and sat in the cockpit. "Here I am," I said.

He came up the ladder from the main cabin slowly and warily. When his head appeared, he paused to inspect the cockpit first. He was a mess. Joab hadn't shaved, hadn't changed his clothes, either. His shirt was dirty and wrinkled. He looked old and tired. Also, he was holding a bottle of vodka in one hand and a revolver in the other.

"Fucking guns," I said. "This place is filled with fucking guns. Where'd that one come from?"

"It's Freeport Junior's. Thinks he's a damn cowboy. I took it out of his room this morning."

"Well, put it down. It makes me nervous."

"No, I won't do that," he said.

"Then I might as well leave."

"I don't intend to harm you, McFarland."

"I never thought that. But I'm worried about you, Joab," I said. "You're taking this mighty hard."

He used his teeth to unscrew the cap on the vodka bottle and took a big swig. "Damn if it doesn't feel good to drink again out in the open," he said. "I'm on my second bottle of this shit since last night."

"You look it," I said. "What's happening, Joab? What the hell's going on here?"

"Well, number one, I'm drunk. I hold it pretty well, but I'm damned drunk."

"I can see that."

"Number two, I killed Bitsy this morning."

"Christ, don't tell me that."

He took another drink. "It's the truth."

"Then spare the rest of the family and give yourself up.

Chief Simmons is standing right down there on the lawn."

He looked at me in disbelief for a moment, then laughed in my face. "I haven't got to number three. Number three, I'm going to kill myself after we talk."

"Jesus, I don't need this."

"Then you shouldn't have signed on for the cruise, boy," he said. "Bang, bye. That's where I'm coming from. Or going to, as the case may be."

"Why, Joab? We both know that woman thought the world of you," I said. For some strange reason I felt fairly comfortable sitting on the boat talking with him this way.

He laughed again, almost a cough, almost a sob. " 'You always hurt the one you love,' " he said. "Remember that old song? You're old enough."

"Yes, I do," I said.

" 'You always take the sweetest rose and crush it until the petals fall.' Isn't that the way it goes?"

"I think so. Look, at least knock off the booze. If you're going to do these terrible things, at least have possession of your senses when you do them."

He winked at me and drank from the bottle again. "I know what I'm doing, don't worry about that. Besides, that's the dumbest fucking thing I ever heard you say."

"Dumb or not, I meant it."

"Liquor lends false courage, Mac. Don't you know that? Most of the gunfights in the Old West, at least one of the participants was dead drunk. I'm not a brave man. In fact, I'm a coward. So I need the booze. Boy, do I." He took another drink.

"Joab, I loved Bitsy, too. Or I thought I did. A long time ago."

"Oh, I know all about that little mini-affair you two had back in Chicago." He paused. "She told me almost everything, you know. Sooner or later. We had very few secrets, very few." He looked at me. "She told me she had to have an abortion after you, for example. That's an example of how close we were. Very few secrets."

"I never knew that until she told me earlier this week," I said. "I would have married her, Joab."

"Would you now?"

"She thought I was too young for her. I probably was. Of course, you don't know those things at the time."

"I would have married her, too. Except she wouldn't have me, either. Why can't men see these things at the time? Why are we such fools? Will you tell me that? Women have definite goals in life. You didn't see it, and neither did I."

"Maybe she didn't, either. In any event, we have something in common, don't we?"

"No, I don't think you understand, Mac. It happened to you once. With me it got to be a habit."

"But it was so apparent that she loved you, Joab. Anybody could see that."

"Not the way I wanted her to love me," he said, and took another drink. "Like an ugly puppy. Not bought, not from the dog pound, either. A street puppy found shivering in the rain, that was me, brought in out of charity, kept out of pity, always there to come running and offering love when it was needed. And it was. Bitsy had her off moments, believe me."

"Maybe you were the love of her life and she didn't know it," I said.

"Don't try to humor me. But I like the thought. In fact, I'll drink to it." He did. For a man who was supposed to be off the booze for years, he had a great capacity for it. He was drunk and knew it, but still under control, more or less.

"You're something, Joab," I said. "You really are."

"Once. Almost. I think," he said. "If she had let it happen. It was not long after her husband died, dear Freeport, the man who hired me right out of Henry Grady J School. She and I were working night and day to keep the paper going and to put the company together. We just sort of fell in together. We fit, you know. People fit now and then, and she and I did."

"That's the way it was with me, more or less. Accidental," I said. "She was something to look at back then, wasn't she?"

He shook his head as if he were trying to cast off a great weariness. "God, I was happy," he said. "I had it all, my friend. No great newspaper editor, not really, and an ugly little fucker, yet there I was with the best job in the world and the most beautiful woman in the world in love with me."

"At the same time. Most people are never that lucky," I said. "I never have been."

"As things turn out, I wasn't, either," he said. "It didn't last all that long. I should have known better."

"What happened to you two back then, Joab?"

He smiled grimly. "She married somebody else."

"Hell, I know that. Bitsy told me that. What I mean is, I can't understand it. She should have married you."

"There was always me. Can you understand that? I was

always there. He was the county attorney," Joab said. "A big, good-looking bastard and a big swinging dick down home in those days. He'd screwed half the women in the county—hell, in South Georgia—most of them married. And a nice guy. I liked him, thought of him as a friend. And when he went after Bitsy, she responded."

"That's what I don't understand."

"Bitsy chased a dream, I think."

"Don't we all?"

"Not in her professional life. Privately. And when she'd meet a new man who interested her, she'd think it was her dream come true."

"She told me her dream come true slapped her around."

"He was gone inside of six months. And moved to Atlanta within a year."

"And Bitsy fell back in with you. Am I right?" I said.

"I'll drink to that," he said, and did, from the bottle. "Hell, I welcomed her back. I tried to act cool and formal at first, but that didn't last long. All Bitsy ever had to do with me was snap her fingers. And she knew it."

"I'm that way about a woman right now, hung up," I said. "I know the feeling."

"Then it doesn't surprise you that I let it happen again. That one didn't last very long, either. An old college friend of Freeport's and a mistake from the beginning."

"And, as usual, you were there to pick up the pieces."

"You know about this latest one?"

"She was anxious that you not be told, Joab. Not just yet."

182

"A friend called. He assumed I knew."

We stared at each other.

"Go ahead, finish your sentence," he said.

"What?"

"Now you can understand why. Isn't that what you were about to say before you caught yourself?"

I stood and paced about the boat deck. "Okay, she shit on you again and again and was about to do it again. I grant you that," I said. "But you don't kill somebody for that."

"You don't? I did," he said.

"And you fucked up!" I screamed at him.

Joab was crying silently. Tears were running down his cheeks, but he made no move to wipe them away. "God, I loved her, Mac," he said. "As much now as I ever did, always did. I didn't mean to kill her. I swear to God."

"It sounds like an old Dick Powell movie," I said. "Spare me, please."

"It was a phone call from an old business acquaintance, just inquiring," he said. "That's how I learned she was planning to get married again. Afterward, I made a bee-line for the liquor cabinet, and I drank all night. I was sitting on the back porch, still at it, when she came out this morning to go swimming."

"And you confronted her? You asshole, Joab. She had the right to live her life in her own way, too. You denied her that."

"Sit down and quit preaching to me," he said, and I obeyed. "Yes, I confronted her. And she didn't even try to deny it. She tried to tell me what a nice guy this man

183

is and how much I was going to like him, and what a capable communications executive he is and how much he was going to help us."

"And all the time your drunken heart was breaking," I said bitterly. "And you were saying to yourself, I'm going to kill her for this?"

"Yes. Yes. The love of my life, Mac. And she knew that. Because I'd told her so. Countless times when we were back together. She knew she was the love of my life. She knew that, Mac."

"What she said to you must have made you very angry, Joab."

"She said she was very sorry if I had got the wrong idea about her feelings for me, is what she said," he said. "And she told me she would always have a warm spot in her heart for me."

"I've got to admit that is pretty bad," I said, thinking of Kate Bingham.

"I was destroyed."

"Because you knew this was the last time, right? You know, you really ought to be telling the police chief all this," I said. "Let me tell him to come down here. He's a very bright, understanding type of guy."

"No!" Joab jumped to his feet. "This is between you and me, McFarland. I thought you understood that."

"Okay, okay. Sit back down, will you? I'm sorry."

"The thing is, you and I both knew her, you see."

"It's just that I think a good case can be made here for temporary insanity."

"Well, you're right about that."

184

"What did you say to her after she told you she'd always have a warm spot in her heart for you?"

"Nothing, not another word. Then she said she felt like going for a morning swim. I sat there on the porch, spaced out, had another drink, watched her walk across the lawn down to the swimming dock. And went crazy. I guess you're right. Temporarily insane. I jumped up, ran off the porch, across the lawn—"

"And into the wild blue yonder," I said.

"No, deep inside me I knew what I was doing. Or what I was about to do. I wanted to hurt her, punish her. How could she not know what she was doing to me? All that sort of good stuff. Otherwise, I wouldn't have paused long enough to grab one of those croquet mallets, would I?"

"Is that what you hit her with? Jesus, Joab, I simply can't imagine doing that."

"No? Then you haven't been through it long enough yet. I felt as if I was on a mission in a way. Perfectly justified. I felt as if she had driven me to it, but I also felt that she fully deserved it. I was delivering justice. I was declaring my freedom, my deliverance, getting even."

"You were also drunk out of your mind. Liquor fucks a man's brains up, Joab. You know that."

"I'm not trying to defend my actions for a single second, McFarland. I know what I did was wrong, a mortal sin. I'm only trying to explain to you how a person such as you and me can do such a terrible thing. And I know it was a terrible, unforgiving thing."

"So you caught up with her," I said.

"Just as she stepped into the water, down there. She

1 8 5

hadn't heard me coming. Her back was to me, and she'd just taken off her robe. That's when I hit her with the mallet. As hard as I could. And God help me, God damn me, for a single second, when I did it, it felt good. Do you hear what I'm saying?" He was shouting and didn't know it. "When I felt the mallet drive into her head, it felt good for a brief moment. The woman I loved. It felt good. Payback for all those years when I was waiting for her to love me the way I loved her. Can you possibly understand that?"

"Almost," I said. "How many times? That's important to me. I mean, did you stand there, pounding on her?"

"Once!" he cried. "Christ! I was amazed the second I did it. I could never have hit her again. Mac, it only felt good for a second. Then I was horrified by what I had done."

"Well, once proved to be enough," I said. "Cyril said he pulled her body out of the water. Did you throw her in after you hit her?"

"When I hit her, she took a step or two and tumbled into the marsh grass. Her back was to me. I don't think she knew it was me."

"And what did you do?" I asked coldly. "Run away? Back to your bottle?"

He glared at me, then looked away in shame. "No, when I realized what I'd done, I jumped in the water after her. Waist deep, that's all. She was dead. I'd killed her with a single blow. When I realized that, that's when I ran away, back to my bottle, as you put it."

"I hate you, you bastard," I said.

"Far less than I hate myself."

"Don't you dare try to give me that self-serving crap!" I shouted. "You took another human being's life. It was not an accident. You did it on purpose, you asshole. And here you are, trying to explain it away. Well, you can't, Joab. There are some things you can't explain away."

"No pity, Mac?"

"Not one ounce!" I shouted. "Do you expect any? Maybe from some saint, but that's not where I'm coming from."

"No, I really didn't expect pity from you," he said. "I know how you felt about Bitsy."

"Good. Because you're not getting any."

"But because you knew her so well, I did expect a little understanding, I suppose."

"Fuck you, Joab!" I yelled. "I'm weary to the bone of bastards like you who take matters into their own hands, screw things up, and then say poor me, I was driven to do it. It's not really my fault. The hell it wasn't your fault. She'd be alive if you hadn't killed her. You leaned on Bitsy as if she were your personal crutch, and when that crutch broke, you blamed her and not yourself. The crutch wasn't strong enough, was it?"

"You're right," he said helplessly. "Now get off this boat."

"Not quite yet."

For the first time he pointed the gun at me. "Yes, this very second. I'm sick of it all." He took another big drink from his bottle. "Get off the boat now, Mac."

"You're crazy, Joab."

"Probably."

"I'm not leaving you. I will not do that. I think we ought

187

to talk some more. I've still got a lot of unanswered questions." Noah had been watching us closely, needless to say, with his revolver drawn, and I could see that he was slowly inching his way closer and closer to the boat. Joab didn't seem to notice.

He finished the rest of the vodka and threw the empty bottle over the side into the water. "What questions? You know everything," he said.

"Bitsy confessed to me that she killed Peter Stallings. Did you know that? Were you in on it with her?"

"Bitsy told you that?" he cried. "And you believed her? Christ, I thought you knew the woman, McFarland. She didn't do it. I did it. I killed Peter Stallings."

"I'm not sure I believe you."

"As God is my witness, McFarland."

"Are you saying you argued and then you killed him before you left the boat that night?"

"Nothing of the kind. We argued. I left the boat, went up and sat on the back porch for a while, with a drink I poured myself from the bar. And the longer I sat, the madder I got. So I decided to go back down there and have it out with him again. But when I got back here on the boat, I found the bastard passed out, gun on the table. It was too good an opportunity to pass up. So I blew him away." He stood up. "I know there's more vodka down in the cabin. If you want to talk, you'll have to sit here and wait until I round up a new bottle." He quickly climbed down into the main cabin again.

Noah moved quickly, to within a few feet of the boat, but I held my hand up to prevent him from coming aboard. "Come on, Joab," I called out.

"Hold your horses. I can't find the damn liquor cabinet." He gave a short laugh. "So you thought Bitsy did it, did you?"

"That's what she told me."

"Well, she didn't have anything to do with it. And neither did Sally Ann. Or anybody else but me. I killed him. Me alone."

Noah was aboard the boat. "Shh," he whispered.

"Boy, that Bitsy. She was something else, wasn't she?" we heard Joab say.

Then we heard the cruel, sharp sound of the gun.

16

IT WAS AS IF those left at Belle Haven were the stunned survivors of a nuclear blast. They knew something horrible and obscene had happened, something that would change the course of their lives forever, but the devastation had left them numb and altered.

Sally Ann, as if she were a madwoman playing with her rag dolls, played croquet with her two children.

Polly sat in a canvas-backed chair on the gazebo and contemplated Clam Pond. Every now and then she bent forward from the waist and buried her face in her hands.

Her husband Cyril sat on the back porch in a cataonic state, staring across the lawn at his grieving wife.

Freeport Junior paced about the place, searching for a way to express his feelings. "Oh, how very few days we are destined to spend on our mother planet," he declared at one point.

Noah arranged for the bodies to be released for burial, and I had them flown by commercial jet to Brunswick, Georgia. I rode down with the family on the company plane, then rented a car in Brunswick and followed their limousine and the hearse to the family farm in Freeport, about twenty miles away.

Bitsy was buried beside her husband Freeport under the shade of a live-oak tree in the old family plot at the farm. Joab Wolfe had no living relatives, so they decided, perhaps out of desperation and perhaps because of some abiding love for the man, to bury him in a faraway corner of the same plot. "I truly believe it would have been what Mother Bitsy wanted," declared Freeport Junior, whose sudden and somewhat startling proposal it was. "Besides, he surely did not knoweth what he did." The love-starved man who had crushed their stepmother's skull with a croquet mallet was laid to rest about twenty yards away from her grave. Southern Gothic, a story for future generations. I kept my mouth shut through it all.

Afterward we ate cheese grits, salty country ham, and cantaloupe slices, and nobody voiced any objection when Freeport Junior announced that he had arranged for representatives of both the Gannett and Newhouse publishing companies to meet with them to discuss terms for a possible sale of the company. I knew it was as good as done.

I said my good-byes with the distinct feeling that they did not regret to see me go and drove back to Brunswick, to the municipal airport at Glencove, an old, deactivated naval air station that once housed sub-hunting blimps. From there I caught a Delta commuter flight, which put me into Atlanta at four that afternoon. I had a connecting flight to Boston an hour later, but I didn't take it. Instead I caught another Delta flight to Mobile.

Maybe it was because too many people had been too eager to confess to the murder of Peter Stallings. Also, there was something, something Joab Wolfe had said on that boat, although I couldn't put my finger on it. Something compelled me to pay Miss Second Place Alabama a surprise visit.

At Dannelly Field in Mobile I rented a Hertz compact and, at an airport pay phone, called the first television station listed in the Yellow Pages.

"Channel Five," the operator said.

"This is the Freeport Communications station, isn't it?"

"No, sir. That's WFRE. We're on Government Street. They're over on Broadcast Drive. Would you like the number?"

When she answered her phone at WFRE, Miss Second Place Alabama sounded rather like a wife calling home to check up on a husband in bed with a cold. "Darling?" she said.

"Miss Darling, you don't know me. . . ."

She gave a deep sigh. "Please, sir, I get calls from common viewers such as you all the time since I became weekend anchor here. You'll have to excuse me, please." Her accent was a blend of sweet-potato pie and banana pudding, with whipped-cream topping. "Just because I'm blond with blue eyes and all," she added.

"I'm not from Mobile, Miss Darling," I said. "I'm well beyond the reach of your station's transmitter. I'm from Cape Cod, Massachusetts."

"Oh," was all she said to that. Talking about your pregnant pauses, she was about eight months gone.

"We have a mutual friend there, I believe. Did have," I said. "I think you know who I mean."

"Oh. I see," she said. She sounded as if she was scared shitless to me, which was the general effect I was aiming for.

"I think we should get together for a talk," I said.

"No. I'm sorry, but that would be impossible," she said quickly, a note of panic in her voice. "Now you will have to excuse me, as I have a story to prepare and as I am on a deadline. . . ."

"After you're off the air, then?"

"You're some sort of family representative, aren't you?"

"I'm a family friend, yes, but not their representative."

"What is this, a payoff or something?"

"The Binford family doesn't even know I'm in Mobile, Miss Darling."

"Because I'm not for sale, Mr. Whatever Your Name Is. I'm just a country girl and proud of it, thank you very much," she said defiantly.

"My name's McFarland," I said, speaking quickly because I could sense she was spooked and might hang up on me. "I'm just a friend of your friend," I lied. "Who knows a few things that might interest you."

"I really don't know what you're talking about."

"Listen, I was close to Peter Stallings," I said. Working as an investigative reporter really teaches a person how to lie.

"Peter told you about he and I?" she asked in an incredulous tone of voice.

193

"In fact, sad to say, I was the one who first discovered poor Peter's body, I'm afraid."

She sighed, a sigh of resignation. "I guess I knew somebody like you would show up. I fibbed, Mr. McFarland. I'm not on the air tonight. I could meet you."

"You won't be sorry. Please suggest someplace, as I am not familiar with your beautiful city." Drink the wine and speak the language of the country, that was always my motto.

"I suppose my place. I live in a condo. Two two two Bayfront Drive. It's over in Daphne, on the eastern shore."

"I'll find it. See you around eight, okay?" I hung up before she had a chance to think about it anymore.

I had a little time, and I had never been in Mobile before, so, using the Hertz city map, I took a ride around the town. Mobile, I discovered, is every bit as pretty and as picturesque as Charleston or Savannah. Located inside Mobile Bay, where the waters of Alabama's rivers run into the Gulf of Mexico, old Mobile has a French-Spanish aura about it, a town of big houses with double porches, of shady streets lined with live-oak trees draped with moss, and, I decided that August afternoon, a town whose heat and humidity level is exceeded only by that of the steam room in the Chicago YMCA.

Bayfront Drive obviously was a yuppie haven, and 222 had a nice water view. Pretty elegant digs, even for a weekend anchor who had to fend off common viewers.

When she opened her front door for me, I saw why. There she was, Miss Swanee River, Miss Boll Weevil, Miss Ol' Miss. There she was, every juicy, long-limbed cheerleader lusted after in every stadium by every beer-sotted fan, every homecoming queen on every float since they invented the game of football, every beauty contestant who ever paraded down a runway. Also, she didn't look glitzy or trashy, as I somehow had expected she would. She looked sweet, simple, and very, very young.

She was barefoot, dressed in faded jeans and a T-shirt.

"Sue Alice, what a real pleasure it is to meet you at long last. I'm Mac McFarland," I said as we shook hands.

"Hi nice to meet yew," she said in an accent so syrupy you knew that she had grown up deep in rural black-belt Alabama. I wondered how, even in Mobile, they understood what she was saying when she was delivering the news on television.

"I have heard so much about you," I said. If you wanted to be very nice, you would say I was feeling my way. Groping, in other words.

"All nice things I hope," she said, blushing, of course.

"Great things. Except Peter understated the case," this old smoothie replied.

"You know, it's funny, Mr. McFarland. Peter never once mentioned your name to me. As I recall," she said.

"Well, I was just another guy, after all. But you were the love of his life."

"Please come in," she said.

Her condo was nicely furnished, but with new things, nothing personal, not a photograph, not even the child's beauty-contest trophies, at least not in the living–dining room. "Nice place," I said.

"You like it? Thank you. Peter picked everything out. Please sit down."

I did, in an overstuffed chair that almost swallowed me.

"Mr. McFarland, you don't know what that means to me," she said.

"What does exactly?"

"Why that Peter told you I was the love of his life," she said. "He did tell you that?"

"Why, of course." I felt like a dirty dog because my lie had brought tears to her china-blue eyes.

She sniffed. "We were going to get married, you know."

No, I didn't. "When?" I asked.

"The second he and his wife got divorced. She made Peter so unhappy, Mr. McFarland. But I guess I don't have to tell you that, do I?"

"I'm sorry, Sue Alice. Really," I said.

"What might have been. The saddest words ever uttered by tongue or pen," she said.

Close. I was beginning to get the feeling that Sue Alice was another in the long list of Peter Stallings's emotional victims. "How old are you, anyway?" I asked her.

"Twenty-four. Next week."

"Were you really Miss Second Place Alabama?"

She gave me a smile. "Oh yes indeed. When I was nineteen."

"Those must have been happy days for you."

"I whistled," she said.

"You what?"

"In the talent competition. I whistled." She pursed her lips and whistled for me. A few bars of "Stardust." "My daddy taught me how," she said.

"How long did you know Peter?" I asked this whistling child-woman. I mean, she did have this body.

"We met when I first joined WFRE three years ago, right out of college. I was a J school major."

"I'm sure it must have been overwhelming, the big boss making a play for you."

"Oh, he swept me off my feet," she said. "I admit it. He was so handsome and distinguished. He was the company president, after all, and there I was, a beginning street reporter still wet behind the ears professionally." She blushed. "And inexperienced! Let me tell you. I told you I'm a country girl."

"Okay, just don't try and tell me you didn't have lots of boyfriends in high school and college, Sue Alice. You're too pretty not to have had."

"One. Bobby Zanes. All the way through high school and college. Until I met Peter, really. We were pinned in college. We were going to get married. Until Peter and I met."

"Maybe you and Bobby Zanes can get back together now."

"Maybe," she said. "If he gets divorced, which I doubt he will, because I'm told he loves that new baby daughter of his to death."

"Well, you're young. You'll put all this behind you."

"I know I'll never really be in love again." She dabbed at her eyes.

"I guess everybody in the newsroom knew about you two," I said.

"Everybody at the station. Every engineer, every secretary in the business office. Nobody ever said a word to me. But I knew they all knew. When they gave me the weekend anchor job, I went in and looked the news director straight in the eye. Is this promotion because of Peter Stallings? I asked him that directly. He swore it wasn't, that I'd earned it. But now I wonder."

"What's your situation there now?"

"I've been fired."

"Just like that?"

"Well, not exactly. The word's not out yet, not that it will take very long. The news director called me in a couple of days ago and told me I should start sending my tapes around to other stations, because they won't be renewing my contract. He said a cutback. I've got about two months to find another job."

"And you think the family's behind it?"

"Who else?"

"According to what I was told, the family thought you and Peter were an item out of the distant past, that it was long over."

Sue Alice looked at me in amazement. "Look around this place," she said, opening her arms. "It cost much more than I ever could afford on the twenty-five thousand they pay me. Peter bought and furnished it for us." She led me from the living room into the master bedroom and opened a closet door. "Peter's wardrobe," she said. "Suits, shirts, shoes, the works. Jeans, sweatshirts. Do you want to see his medicine in the bathroom cabinet?"

"I don't think so," I said. We went back into the living room. You could see the lights of the city and the shipping traffic in the bay from her big picture window. "He, well, lived here when he was in town?" I asked. "I mean, he was that open about it?"

"Sometimes he slipped in for a private visit, and it was

almost like we were married. When he was here on company business, he took a suite at the Admiral Simms but stayed here overnight."

"And you thought he was going to marry you?"

"I knew he was going to marry me," she insisted.

I took her hands in mine. "I hate to be the one to say this to you, but Peter had a way of using people sometimes, and using them pretty badly."

"He wasn't using me!" she cried. "He loved me! He told me so again and again."

"He told you he was going to divorce his wife, too. But did he ever make one serious move in that direction?"

"He was about to," she said. She was standing at her picture window, looking out at Mobile Bay. A pretty girl, a nice girl, a nice slightly-below-medium-bright girl.

"About a year ago, when Bitsy Binford found out about you and Peter, she confronted him. She told him she would fire him if he didn't end his relationship with you. Did he ever tell you that?"

She shook her head. "No. He said we had to cool it for a while because the word was getting out in the company prematurely about he and I. But he never said a word about Mrs. Binford threatening to fire him." She shook her head in despair. "I don't know about any of this," she moaned.

I walked over and put my arm around her shoulder. "You were in over your head, Sue Alice. Peter was a very sick and confused man when you met him."

"I don't know what's happening, except everybody's getting killed, and I didn't have anything to do with it," she wailed. "You said you discovered his body. We heard it was suicide at the station, but I can't believe that. Tell me, please, what's happening?"

I led her over to the couch, and we sat beside each other. "I'm trying to figure it out, too, Sue Alice. Will you try and help *me*?"

"I'll try."

"You two talked frequently?"

"Every day. About our marriage plans."

Christ, she was dumb as a post. "Peter didn't have any marriage plans, Sue Alice. What did he tell you?"

"He kept saying he needed more time."

"And you were beginning to hound him. More and more. Weren't you?"

She wiped her wet cheeks with the back of her bare hand. "I was on his case there at the end. I admit that."

"I don't blame you," I said. "You were beginning to realize he was leading you on." I paused, let her think. "So you two talked the night Peter died," I suggested.

"Yes," she said. "At least, I think we did. From what I can figure out. Nobody has said a word to me about all this until this very minute, you understand."

"You argued."

More tears. "I didn't mean for him to go and kill himself. I swear I didn't."

"What did you talk about? Do you remember any details?"

She hesitated. "I don't know you very well."

"Please trust me. What choice do you have?"

She looked down at her bare feet. "Well, Peter liked to talk about sex," she said.

"Lots of men do."

"I mean really talk about it. In detail, you know."

"I know. I mean, I understand. What I mean is, I don't like to do that myself, but I understand."

She still would not face me. "I never liked it especially. But I was so young and inexperienced when we first met, well, I thought, this must be how it is." Finally she looked at me. "Is it?"

"Not with everybody. With some."

"He liked to talk nasty to me. Really, really nasty. He'd tell me to do things with my hands to myself, which I wouldn't, of course, but I'd lie and pretend and say I was doing it, you know?"

"I know," I said.

"He seemed to enjoy it so, so I went along with it."

"Don't worry about it, Sue Alice," I said.

"I didn't feel comfortable with it. But he sounded so urgent. Frantic, even, at times."

"He was a pretty frantic man along about then. More than you knew probably," I said.

She gave her feet another close examination. "That's not all. He made me talk to him. Talk dirty, Mr. McFarland." She put her face in her hands. "And I mean dirty, dirty. God, I was brought up in the Southern Baptist Church. My parents would die if they ever found out. And our pastor back home in Tunnel Springs, who's the sweetest thing that ever lived, it'd kill him, too."

"Unless you tell them, they'll never know," I said. I waited a moment and let her compose herself. "Was that the way it was that last night?" I asked.

"Yes. After the dirty talk he quieted down. 'I love you so.' I remember he told me that."

"Think hard about this. Did he threaten to kill himself during your talk?"

"No, no he didn't," she said immediately.

"Not a word about suicide?"

"The subject never came up. We argued. I told him he had to free himself from that fanatical woman."

"Exactly what did he say to that? Do you remember?"

"I'll never forget it," she said. "He said, 'Sometimes I wonder if it's ever going to work out for us, darling.' He called me darling."

"Did he tell you why it wasn't going to work out?"

"Sally Ann's a fanatical Catholic, as you know. Goes to mass every day, rain or shine."

"I don't know how devout she is. I know they had a Catholic wedding."

"Peter said Sally Ann told him she would never agree to a divorce, only to an annulment," Sue Alice said. "Which, he so correctly pointed out, because I did a report on it because we have so many Catholics here in Mobile, is almost impossible to get after there are children."

"So Peter said he'd talked to Sally Ann about a divorce and she said she would never agree?" I asked. "What did you tell him?"

The feet got another once-over. "That's when I told him I'm pregnant," she said.

I sat there and looked at her.

"Two months," she said. "The last time he was here."

I still didn't say anything.

"He hung up on me. Never said a word. Just hung up

on me. I sat in this very room and cried for over an hour."

"He never tried to call you back?"

"No."

"So you sat here."

"I had a glass of wine. I know I shouldn't have, but I did. It doesn't take much for me."

"If anybody ever needed a drink, I guess it was you," I said.

"It didn't help. Not one bit. I felt like the world was coming to an end," she said.

"You were a brave girl," Old Dad here said, feeling as if I were talking to a Girl Scout who had just earned a merit badge in rock climbing or something, except this one had a little Brownie in the oven.

"That's why, when you contacted me so unexpectedly this afternoon, at first I thought the family had sent you," she said.

"That puzzled me," I told her. "You said something about a payoff. What did you mean by that?"

I thought at first that she had gone catatonic on me. But after a long silence, looking at me and not at her feet this time, she said, "I called her."

Finally I knew why I had come to Mobile. "You called . . . Sally Ann?" I asked.

"I knew Peter was on his new boat. He told me he was sleeping there alone to keep away from her. So I got the number at their house from the long-distance operator."

"That must have been quite a conversation the two of you had," I said. I felt dizzy. Not a drop to drink, and I felt dizzy all of a sudden.

"After all that time, it was the first time I'd ever talked to his wife, you know. Actually, the first time I'd ever heard her voice." She smiled a very wan smile at me.

"And you told her? What exactly did you tell Sally Ann, Sue Alice?"

"A mouthful. I mean, she got a mouthful from me that night."

"You told her that Peter loved you and wanted and deserved a divorce."

"Yes. I did."

"And you told her you were pregnant."

"Yes. That's why I thought you'd come to offer me a payoff or something. To keep me quiet."

"No. There's no longer any need for you to keep quiet, Sue Alice," I told her.

17

◊ THE LAST WEEK of August was the best of that summer, and when I returned to the Cape from my Southern voyage of discovery, I was determined to take a little time off.

Noah took me scuba diving. We sped down to Vineyard Sound in his Boston Whaler and spent a day swimming around the wreckage of the *Sagamore,* a centerboard schooner that sank in 1907 after a collision with a Norwegian steamer. That was fun, swimming with all the fish and watching big lobsters peer at you through the ship's portholes.

Bascombe and I watched television sports. In his den at home we watched Joe Morgan's Red Socks hobble toward the end of a mediocre season, and at the Binnacle we watched the Patriots get clobbered by the Buffalo Bills. Bascombe's prediction was that the Celtics weren't going to be all that good, either.

Terry Riley, back on his feet, told me all about his plans for an open house to celebrate the completion of the renovation of St. John's parochial school while I drank his white wine and he cooked us curried fish soup with cream and tomatoes for lunch. We ate the soup with big croutons he made with slices of French bread and declared it good, very good, three bowlfuls good.

I also took long, solitary walks along Nauset Beach and did not think about Kate Bingham. Make that tried not to think about her.

The Labor Day weekend arrived, and North Walpole was choked with its traffic.

Cape Cod no longer tucks itself in for the season immediately after Labor Day the way it once did. Most of the shops and restaurants now remain open at least until Thanksgiving. But Labor Day still brings a change in tempo. Suddenly the beaches are less crowded, and the line of customers at the fish market is not so long. Many of the larger boats anchored in Pilgrim Harbor leave for warmer waters south, down the Intercoastal Waterway to Fort Lauderdale and beyond. Noah Simmons terminates the police-force temporaries he hires to cope with summer crowds, and North Walpole's public-school bells ring. The town's throttle is pulled back to half-speed.

I was still living at Belle Haven, in an empty house, living on microwaved TV dinners, scrambled eggs, and instant coffee. The house had been abandoned when the Binford family rushed home to Freeport in such haste and emotional confusion. Bitsy's things were still there. I didn't touch them.

At the end of the first week of September I called the farm in Freeport and talked with Lily Dell. She told me Sally Ann was busy getting her two children back in school, Polly was busy escorting Cyril Theobald back and forth to daily sessions with a psychiatrist in Jacksonville, and Mr. Baby was back in Houston, where, no doubt, he was trying to ward off creditors. Lily Dell also told me that I should feel free to stay on at Belle Haven for as long as I wanted, and she told me where I could find Bitsy's address book with all the names and numbers of the people she hired for household and groundskeeping help.

Armed with that, I proceeded to close down most of the house for the winter. I had the dock taken out of the water and stacked on the lawn. I dismantled the miniature-golf course and the croquet court and stashed the equipment in the garage, missing one red mallet I assumed was still in Noah's possession. The gardeners and the house cleaners had worked for Bitsy for years, so I stood by and watched while they did their work.

The Saturday afternoon open house at St. John's was a happy and crowded occasion. There was enough food to have fed Patton's army for a week, and the renovated school sparkled and shined in the warm September sun. I didn't think I had ever seen Terry Riley so happy.

When I got back to Belle Haven, it was midafternoon, and Sally Ann was there. She was sitting on the back porch in Bitsy's wicker chair, drinking a vodka and tonic she had made for herself. I didn't know why she had returned to North Walpole, but I was not surprised at all to see her there. It was as if I had been expecting to see her show up this way, casually and without prior notice.

"Lily Dell told me you were staying here, taking care of things," she said, raising her glass when I walked out on the porch. "For which I thank you. We all went rushing off in such confusion and panic. I left half my things in the new addition."

"I could have sent them to you," I said.

"To tell you the truth, I wanted to come back and take a look at this place. Where it all happened."

"Is everything all right with you?" I asked. I hadn't spoken to her since my talk with Sue Alice Darling. I had told no one about that conversation, not even Noah. I was sick and tired of the whole affair, and I knew there was no way Noah could prove Sally Ann had blown her beloved husband's brains out of his fair-haired head. Murders that are never solved are committed all the time is what I told myself.

"Everything is fine, really," she said. "I've packed some things you can have UPS pick up and send home collect, if you will. I've got a taxi coming in a few minutes to take me to Hyannis, and the company plane's waiting for me there."

"Speaking of the company . . ."

"The deal's all set. Newhouse is paying us a fortune for it."

I didn't say anything to that.

"Look, with Peter and Mother Bitsy and Joab all gone, there really was nobody left who knew how to run it," she said. "Besides, we all come out of it rich. And that's all Polly and Freeport Junior ever really wanted."

"Mr. Baby didn't object? I thought he might like trying to play publisher for a while."

She smiled at that. "He was happiest of all. His share gives him enough to pay off all his debts and live the high old life for a while."

"Lily Dell told me he's gone back to Houston."

"To try to get his wife to come back to him," she said. "Also, he has a new toy. The *Comchi*. He gets it as part of the sale agreement, and he intends to have a professional crew sail it around Key West to Houston. To show off to all his friends. Can't you just see that silly thing?"

"Isn't it hurricane season pretty soon?"

"Mac, you know nobody can preach a word of sense to that boy, never could."

"Lily Dell told me Cyril was seeing some psychiatrist in Jacksonville," I said.

"Cyril hasn't spoken a word aloud to anyone since Mother Bitsy's death. He communicates only with Polly, and only with a tablet and pencil. And even then, very infrequently. They've moved home, into the big house. Cyril just sits in a bare room, staring at his typewriter. He doesn't even jog anymore. Can you imagine?"

Somehow I didn't think the world would be the less for all of that. "The help? Are they all right?"

"Lily Dell and Lincoln will stay on at the farm until they both die, of course. Wyvonny's talking about moving to Atlanta. She says there's greater opportunity there. Whatever that means."

"What about you, Sally Ann? What about your future?"

"Oh my, I'll end up as the old stay-at-home, I'm sure. Not that I don't have plenty to keep me busy. Two children to raise. A family tradition to uphold."

"You were talking about traveling around the world the last time we talked."

"But that was before Mother Bitsy was . . . passed away. I have added responsibilities now. Don't you worry about me. Freeport can be a gay old place at times. I've got my garden-club work and my church work both to keep me busy. Not to mention those two children."

I took a deep breath. "Sally Ann, after I left Freeport, I went to Mobile to see Sue Alice Darling."

"That little whore. Whatever for?" she asked quickly.

"I thought she was a pretty nice young woman, actually," I said.

"You didn't know her."

"I don't think you did, either."

"I know she tried to take my husband away from me. I know that about her."

I frowned, pretending to be puzzled by her remark. "I thought you and Peter worked that out."

"Well, actually we did. But I never forgot it. Can you blame me for that?"

"He never broke up with her, did he? And you knew it."

She sighed. "Well, I suspected it."

"What made you suspicious, Sally Ann?"

"Well, he was gone so much, for one thing. So much travel. Peter was constantly on the road."

"Sue Alice Darling wasn't the bad person, Sally Ann. Peter Stallings was. You know that, don't you?"

"No."

"She was an impressionable young girl when he first met her. Just as you were when you first met him. And he took advantage of that."

"She was a whore. His whore."

"He lied to her the same way he lied to you, Sally Ann. He led her on. He told her he loved her."

"She was his whore."

2 1 0

"He told her he wanted to marry her, except you wouldn't agree to a divorce. In fact, he never asked you for one, did he?"

"He asked for one, then told me he'd changed his mind. He said he wanted us to try and work it out."

"And he got her pregnant. You know that. After Peter died, you called the station in Mobile and demanded that they fire her, didn't you?"

"And what of it?"

"You know, Sally Ann, Peter's death still worries me," I said.

"Peter went over the edge," she said.

"First, Bitsy told me she did it. Then Joab told me no, she didn't, he did it. And God knows he was driving both of them crazy."

"Peter killed himself," she said.

"No, he didn't."

"That's what the police say."

"You of all people know better than that, Sally Ann."

"What do you mean by that? Exactly what do you mean by that?"

"Peter talked to Sue Alice on the boat phone that night. He told her you would only agree to an annulment, which was almost impossible to obtain under the circumstances. And she panicked. She called you. She begged you to give Peter an annulment. She told you she was pregnant with Peter's child, didn't she, Sally Ann?"

She looked at me. Her eyes had filled with tears.

"And it was all news to you, wasn't it?" I said. "You thought the old affair was over, and now you realized it wasn't, hadn't ever ended. You were shocked and angered, and all of Peter's comings and goings suddenly added up, didn't they?"

"You're saying I killed him, aren't you?" she said.

"Yes, I'm afraid I am, Sally Ann. After Joab staggered off the boat that night, thinking he'd been fired with Bitsy's consent, Peter talked with Sue Alice, and after she told him she was pregnant, he hung up on her and hit the cognac bottle, really hit it."

She said nothing.

"After Sue Alice called you, you went down to the boat to confront Peter. But what you found was a crazy, drunken man. Maybe passed out. Am I right?"

Sally Ann sighed, almost as if she were exasperated. "He wasn't passed out," she said. "But drunk and crazy, yes."

"And you realized you didn't love him anymore. You hated him."

She laughed, but it was a short, bitter laugh, almost a cough. "You should have seen him. You should have heard him," she said. "I don't know how much he and Uncle Joab drank together, and I really don't know how much time passed after Uncle Joab left and before I showed up, but my husband was a mess, a ranting, raving mess. Nobody has ever talked to me that way in my life."

"I'm truly sorry, Sally Ann."

"I want to tell you what he said to me. He told me he didn't love me, that he'd never loved me. He told me he hated having sex with me."

"Look, Peter Stallings was a bastard, and a crazy bastard, to boot. You don't have to convince me of that."

She continued as if I hadn't spoken, as if she were

2 1 2

talking to herself. "You know, Southern women, us Southern belles, we think of sex as the last available port in a storm." She looked at me. "Peter hadn't screwed me in a year, you know."

I could believe it, not because I found her so unattractive, but because of all I had learned about that man and the tangled, confused life he led.

"I went to him that night," Sally Ann said. "What a silly thing to have done, honestly. I sat on the couch beside him. I put my arm around him and tried to kiss him. I told him I still loved him." She paused and covered her face with her hands. "I was only wearing my nightgown. Do you want to know what I did? Silly fool, I pulled it up around my waist. I lay back on that damn couch and spread my legs for him. And I begged him to fuck me, Mr. McFarland."

"Ah, shit," I said, despite myself.

"He laughed at me. He pushed me away and turned his head. He told me I'd ruined his life, that he'd married me for all the wrong reasons, that he never really had been attracted to me. That I made his life miserable. Then he stood up and looked down at me lying there. He laughed at me. Who'd want to fuck that? That's what he said to me."

"And what did you do then? The gun was there on the table, wasn't it?"

"No, there wasn't a gun anywhere to be seen. What I did was, I gagged. I could feel the vomit rising suddenly in my throat, so I jumped up and ran into the boat's master bedroom, into the toilet. Where I proceeded to puke my guts out."

"You found the gun in the master bedroom."

She threw her hands up in near-disgust. "No, damn it. Will you please listen to me? Please? I washed my face, rinsed out my mouth with some Scope, and stood there, looking at myself in the mirror. What a sight. I mean, what a sight! I can still remember how I looked. I remember saying to myself, Well, here you are."

She had finished her drink. She placed the empty glass on the rattan table and stood, gazing out at Clam Pond. "The phone rang," she said.

"The cellular phone, there on the boat?"

"Of course, what else? It kept ringing, and I knew, I mean I knew, that it was that Darling whore calling Peter back, and I thought to myself, Well, let her have him."

"I could check with her."

"Check with her. What do I care?"

"What happened next?"

"The damn phone just kept ringing. And ringing. I can't stand that, never could. So finally I walked back into the main cabin. I was going to tell Peter, Well, answer the damn thing." She turned to face me, the pretty summer wife, face still tanned, her hair tied back with a ribbon. "And he was standing there with that gun in his hand. Standing there, listening to that damn phone ring. And had the barrel of the gun stuck in his mouth, Mr. McFarland."

I didn't believe a word of what she was saying, but I didn't tell her that. I was still convinced I had solved myself a murder case, and I wasn't going to let her talk me out of it. Finally I asked, "Did you try to reason with him?"

"You should have seen him, seen his face. If you had, you wouldn't bother to ask that question."

"Well, did you try to get the gun away from him? Was there a struggle? Was it an accident? Is that what you're trying to tell me?"

"No, I . . ." She hesitated. "For some reason he was holding the gun in his left hand."

"His left hand?"

"Yes. For some reason. And that meant, from where I was standing, I'd have to reach across his chest and try to pull it out of his hand, or out of his mouth."

"I understand," I said, and at last I really did.

"I begged him. Please, don't, I said. I said it softly, not in a loud voice at all. And the phone was still ringing. I decided if I could just stop that. So I stepped forward to pick it up . . ."

I thought she had finished talking. "And?" I asked softly.

"And that was when Peter Stallings closed his eyes and blew his brains out," she said.

We stood facing each other, looking into each other's eyes. At last, she stepped forward and laid her head on my chest. "I'm a nice girl, Mr. McFarland," she said. "I know I act bitchy at times, but I'm a nice girl. I'm a good girl."

"You ran off that boat and went flying back to the big house to Bitsy, didn't you?" I asked.

"Yes, I did. That's exactly what I did."

"Where Joab Wolfe was sitting quietly in the dark on the porch. You didn't see him, but he must have heard the shot. And when he saw you running off the boat, he knew something bad had happened. And he knew you were involved."

"I don't know. I never saw him. I was scared out of my wits."

"It's only a guess on my part," I said. "But I do know the last thing he did before he took his own life was try to place all the blame on himself and absolve you and Bitsy."

"Poor Uncle Joab. You know, I always thought Mother Bitsy should have married him."

"Well, you're not the only one," I said. "What did Bitsy do when you told her what had happened?"

"She insisted that we go back to the boat together so she could have a look for herself. I didn't want to do it, but she made me."

"And you found Peter lying there, sprawled on the couch. And still very dead."

She nodded her head. "Yes. Mother Bitsy looked at him and said she had wondered how it would all end up. Then she put her arms around me and hugged me."

"What did she tell you?"

"She told me to play the grief-stricken widow, which I really was, and leave the rest to her." She paused, then added uncertainly, "She told me she would invite you over for coffee that morning. She said there was a way you could be of help in this."

"Well, I certainly did that," I said. "Bitsy immediately took charge, didn't she?"

"You knew her, Mr. McFarland. She told me not to worry about fingerprints, because we'd both been on the boat before, so it was only natural there would be prints."

"Anything else?"

"I remember she told me we both must be very careful and not touch Peter's body. And neither of us did."

"There was one thing you touched, though. Wasn't there? Think about it, Sally Ann," I said.

It didn't take her long. "Oh, you mean the gun," she said. "We couldn't find it at first. It had fallen and slid halfway under the couch. When we did finally find it, Mother Bitsy stuck a ballpoint pen in the barrel and picked it up and put it nearer Peter's hand."

Closer to his right hand, I thought to myself, a right hand whose strength and use had been impaired by a stroke Bitsy obviously had known nothing about at the time, an ignorance that had led her to place the Smith & Wesson revolver close by the wrong hand and that subsequently had led yours truly to a set of wrong conclusions.

Sally Ann Stallings had not known about the stroke, either. She had been telling the truth as only she could have known it when she said her husband held the revolver in his left hand, which had made it impossible for her even to try to wrest it away from him.

It was not a story she had invented, because there was no reason for her to do so. In no way did it provide further proof of her own innocence. Except to me.

Sherlock Holmes strikes again. Ellery Queen solves another tricky one. There had been no murder on that boat. Peter Stallings had killed himself, committed suicide. Noah Simmons's original determination had been the correct one. And if Bitsy Binford had left well enough alone . . .

"Wait a minute," I said. "Sally Ann, there's something you're leaving out, isn't there?"

"What makes you think that?" she asked.

"You forgot how well I used to know Bitsy."

We heard the toot of an automobile horn in the driveway out front. "There's my taxi. Right on time," Sally Ann said. "I've got to scoot."

"Bitsy believed you killed him, didn't she?" I said to her.

She looked at me but didn't speak.

"She certainly acted like it," I said. "Rearranging evidence, covering things up, using me the way she did. She thought you killed Peter, didn't she?"

"Yes, she did," Sally Ann said.

"You see, that explains it."

"I could never convince her otherwise. I told her on the boat that night because I could sense what she was thinking, even though she never accused me outright. Mother Bitsy, I didn't kill him. I didn't do this. He killed himself. I told her that point-blank. She said, I know you didn't, dear. But we must tidy up a little bit."

"That sounds like her. I can hear her saying that," I said.

"I've got to get," she said. "Look, I don't know if anybody has said anything to you. But feel free to stay on here at Belle Haven as long as you'd like. All winter, if that suits you."

I thought about my prospects, which were not very bright, to say the least. "Thanks. What's going to happen to this place, anyhow?"

"Who knows? Your guess is as good as mine."

"What's going to happen to you?"

"Probably nothing very exciting." She smiled at me. "You got any ideas?"

"I know you Southern girls pretty well. You have a talent for survival."

We walked off the porch and through the center hallway of the house. I noticed that she had placed a small bag near the front door. "Well, I'm going home and try to put my life back together. What's left of it," she said. She opened the screened door and waved to the taxi driver. "Yoo-hoo! I'm coming!"

"Bitsy never believed you, did she?" I said. "She always believed you killed him. She tried to convince me that she did it. Trying to protect you. She loved you, Sally Ann."

She picked up her bag, waving aside my offer to help, and smiled at me. A nice girl, a good girl. She leaned forward and kissed me on my cheek. "I know she loved me, as I loved her," she said. "I also know she never believed me. Do you?"

18

DO YOU BELIEVE HER?'' Noah Simmons
asked me the following morning.

I threw my hands up in an admission of defeat.

"Not that it matters one bit," Bascombe Midgeley said.
"The books are closed on that one, believe me."

"I suppose I believe her more than I don't believe her,"
I said. "What about you, Noah?" I had told them Sally
Ann's story in detail.

"Bascombe's right. It's over and done with. History.
Acta est fabula."

"It's mumbo-jumbo time," Bascombe said.

"You were right about the stroke. I'll give you that,"
Noah said.

"Well, my hunch proved right. But it led me to the
wrong conclusion."

"I must say, it's a lucky thing for the bad guys that
you're not a professional law-enforcement officer, Mac,"
Bascombe said.

"Lay off him," Noah said.

"Old cock, I simply was attempting to point out that Mac here solved the Peter Stallings affair two or three different times. That is considerably above and beyond the call of duty."

"And as a lawyer, you know murder probably is the easiest crime to get away with," Noah said. "Mac's suspicions were not unfounded or unreasonable."

"Well, I'm not planning to apply for a private detective's license anytime soon. Or run for county sheriff," I said.

It was a clear and beautiful Sunday morning with a whiff of fall in the air. The three of us were sitting at one of the wooden picnic tables that were placed under the pine trees outside the North Walpole bakery. I was having at a Danish with my coffee, Bascombe was eating his usual croissant with his, and Noah was downing tiger toes, twisted and entwined sugar-cinnamon doughnuts.

The bakery was on the outskirts of town, in a white frame building shaded by a stand of tall pines. During the summer season Sundays were always its busiest days. Sunday mornings you had to take a number from the machine and stand in line to buy the doughnuts and sweet rolls and yeast bread, all warm from the ovens.

The bakery also sold the best coffee in town and the morning papers, Boston and Hyannis, so it was a pleasant place to come and linger, if you could find an empty table. Noah and Bascombe and I always seemed to show up there at about the same time every Sunday morning.

"I wonder what will happen to Belle Haven now," Noah said.

"I know they're selling the company," I said.

"For how much? Do you know?" Bascombe asked.

"To Newhouse. For hundreds of millions."

Noah whistled.

"Newspapers don't come cheap these days," I said. "Not the ones that make money."

"You don't sound too happy about it," Bascombe said.

"Most small-town newspapers that are bought by the chains become bland and predictable," I said. "The new owners are anxious not to offend anybody, because it might cost them advertising."

"Were the Binfords crusaders?" Bascombe asked.

"At least they were Southerners who owned Southern properties. The new owners won't be," I said. "It's happening all over the country, and it worries me. That's all. I guess homogenization is our national destiny."

"What about the Binford family? Will they be coming back to North Walpole or not?" Noah asked.

"Bitsy Binford was the person who held that family together," I said. "I wouldn't be surprised if the place isn't put up for sale sooner or later."

"It can't hold many pleasant memories for them anymore," Bascombe said.

"I'm staying over there," I said. "Probably over the winter."

"I'm sorry about you and Kate, Mac," Bascombe said. "I suppose you know the word's all over town."

"The Binnacle thing?"

"Right down to the brand name of the beer bottle she broke over your head. Narragansett I'm told it was."

Noah reached into his white bakery bag and pulled out his fourth tiger toe. The bag contained his standing Sunday morning order, a sweet fried-dough feast for him and his three growing sons to devour before Dede dutifully dragged them all over to St. Matthew's Episcopal. Noah's wife ran her home and their lives strictly by the book— her book. Her people had lived on Cape Cod for almost as long as her husband's, which was a very long time indeed. She also was Kate Bingham's best friend.

"From what I hear from Boston chums that fellow's quite a catch," Bascombe said. "Kate'll be off to Boston to live, I suppose. When's the wedding?"

She was as close as any sister to both him and Noah, and during better times that year the four of us had been a close social quartet, Binnacle regulars who played darts and drank beer together during the cold, dank months. Bascombe would never admit it, but he didn't want Kate to go away any more than I did.

"About that wedding," Noah said.

"What?" I asked immediately.

"Kate had a talk with Dede. It seems there's not going to be any wedding."

The governor's just granted you a last-minute pardon from the electric chair. Damn good thing our clock here at the state prison's a little slow. That's how I felt.

"Were you going to wait until you'd eaten the very last tiger toe before you told me?" I asked.

"I was getting around to it," he protested.

"She's still snakebitten," Bascombe said. "Always has been and always will be when it comes to men. No offense, Mac. But you are married." He turned to Noah. "What happened? I thought it was a done deal. That was the word."

223

"According to what Kate told Dede, it was a religious thing," Noah said, speaking in a low voice so people sitting at nearby tables couldn't hear him.

"Sounds good so far," I said.

"Anything would, to you, old cock," Bascombe said.

"This Carroll guy's mother is a widow who has a firm grip on the family purse strings and who evidently is a very old-fashioned Irish-Catholic fanatic, mass every day, that sort of thing. Big into all the holy days."

"Then Kate is the perfect daughter-in-law for her," I said.

"The old lady didn't exactly see it that way, I gather. Your rival is an only son, Mac, and extremely close to his mother. Or at least his mother is extremely close to him," Noah said.

"She also obviously is extremely close to the purse, to which she holds the strings," Bascombe murmured.

"Kate thought she'd made a good impression when Carroll took her up to Boston to meet the old lady, so she told Dede. But when he told his mother he planned to marry her, the old lady hit the ceiling, it seems."

"I, too, was an only son," Bascombe said. "Our mothers can be possessive, believe me."

"She had Kate checked out," Noah whispered. "Can you believe that? She learned Kate had been married before and became a widow on her wedding day because of that freak accident."

"A virgin widow. That marriage was never consummated," I said. Bascombe raised his eyebrows to indicate surprise that I possessed such intimate knowledge.

"Which leaves her as good as never married in the eyes of the church," I added. I was angry. It was irrational, but who was this old bat to think Kate wasn't pure enough for her precious sonny?

"That part his mother could live with," Noah said. "At least, she told her son she could, although the fact that the man Kate married wasn't Catholic didn't sit well with her." He paused and looked at me. "What she couldn't live with was you, Mac. The fact that Kate lived with you openly for all these months."

"Well, yes, there is that," I said. Why did it make me feel so good, as if I had saved her? Thank God that old lady had the bulldog tenacity to check into Kate's background so thoroughly.

"She threw a fit over that, evidently, begged and pleaded, screamed and yelled, threatened to leave all her money to the church," Noah said. "She even had some old priest talk with her son and advise against the marriage."

"Well, damn her eyes. Why didn't Carroll just tell the old bitch to go to hell?" I said.

"You're on that old lady's side, aren't you?" Bascombe said.

"I have to admit I admire her for standing fast by her religious beliefs," I admitted. "You got to give her credit for that."

"Kate said Carroll asked her if she would agree to a secret engagement and put off the marriage for the time being, to let things cool down and give him some time to work on his mother and bring her around."

"Not knowing about the full extent of Kate's temper," Bascombe said. "Although I'm sure he found out in a hurry."

"She told him to go to hell in no uncertain terms," Noah said. "We all know her."

"I only wish I could have been there to see it," I said.

"Sound general quarters," Bascombe whispered urgently. He used his copy of the Sunday *Boston Globe* to hide his face and his right thumb to jab toward the bakery's parking lot—where Kate had just pulled up and parked her Honda. She got out of the car and, without looking our way, walked inside the bakery.

"I've got to go home and feed the boys," said Noah, getting up.

"I fear I, too, must make an equally hurried departure," Bascombe said. "Good luck, Mac. Noah and I will come and visit you in the hospital." They both walked quickly to their cars without looking back and drove away.

I sat there and tried to decide how I was going to handle this. I didn't have a clue. About ten minutes later Kate walked out of the bakery carring a small white bag and a plastic coffee cup. A table near the parking lot was empty, and she took a seat there with her back to me. I waited until she had taken a bite of her jelly doughnut and a sip of coffee before I got up and walked over to her. Bullet-biting time.

"You've got to give me this. It's very brave of me to approach you," I said to her back. "You're eating a jelly doughnut, and that means you're saying to hell with everything. Right?"

She turned and looked at me as if I were a total stranger, then said, "Oh, hi, Mac," as if I were the postman. She was wearing her favorite pair of jeans and one of my old shirts, sneakers with no socks, eyeglasses, not her usual contacts, and she had her hair pulled back and tied with a short ribbon.

"Look," I said, eloquently.

"How are you?"

"Okay."

"And how's that wife of yours?"

"Look," I said again, really getting into it.

"I thought you might have got back together. You two look like you were made for each other. Do you know that?"

"Well," I said. "Look." I realized it was not starting out all that well.

"Did you wish something?"

"Yes. I wish to apologize for the way I acted at the Binnacle."

"You should apologize. You were horrible."

"I'm glad you hit me over the head with that beer bottle. It sent me a message."

"You know what I wish? I wish I'd had a baseball bat."

"It was jealousy, Kate. That and too much to drink. Seeing you with that guy blew me away. So, anyhow, I wanted to say I'm sorry."

"I was never so embarrassed in my entire life. Honestly. Screaming to the entire town of North Walpole about what a good screw I am."

"Yes. Look. I want to be especially and extremely apologetic about that particular outburst," I said. "I beg your pardon. Please forgive me. I mean, it's true. You are. But

2 2 7

I am extremely sorry I told everybody in North Walpole."

She looked at me for a long time without saying anything. "You know, don't you?" she said at last. "Noah told you. I saw you sitting here with him and Bascombe."

"Yes, I know. Look."

"I would have married him. Except for that. In a minute. You should know that."

"Kate, I can't believe you were in love with him," I said.

"Women marry men they aren't in love with all the time. Don't you know that? I'm sorry it didn't work out. At first I thought it would."

"Bascombe thinks you're snakebit, and he may be right. Unlucky in marriage, unlucky in this, and God knows unlucky running into me when you did."

"John Carroll would have made me a good husband, and I would have made him a good wife," she said.

"Kate, I never got the chance to tell you that I'm sorry about Earline showing up out of the blue the way she did. Some guy she was hung up with got her hooked on crack. She was here to see if there was any more juice to be squeezed out of my pulp. She won't be back, bothering you." I paused. "I won't, either."

Kate closed her eyes and rested her chin in the palm of her hand with her elbow resting on the tabletop. "Damn it, damn it, damn it all," she said wearily. "Damn you, too."

"Hey, anything it takes," I said, trying my best to smile.

"Don't try to work your charm on me."

I sat down across the table from her. "I'm sort of short-handed in that department these days."

"You think you're so damn charming, don't you?"

"I'm just trying to be nice," I protested. "Give me a break, please."

"Where are you living? In some dump? The way you were when I first met you?"

"Yes," I lied.

"And drinking far too much, the way you were when I first met you. If the spectacle you made of yourself at the Binnacle is any indication."

"I'm doing the best I can," I said. "Getting by."

"John Carroll's mother heard all about that little scene. Somehow. She wrote me a letter. In which she called me your paramour."

"Kate . . ."

"Which I guess I am. Have you found any work? I know you're broke. Or close to it."

"Something'll come up. I'll get by. Don't worry."

"Who's worrying? About you? I'm not the least bit worried about you."

I didn't say anything. I knew better than to open my mouth.

"Well, if you think I'm going to take you back, you're out of your mind," Kate said.

I thought my heart would burst with happiness.

ABOUT THE AUTHOR

DOUGLAS KIKER *is one of the nation's best-known and most widely respected television news correspondents. As a reporter for the* Atlanta Journal, *he observed the turmoil of the Southern civil rights movement. As White House correspondent for the* New York Herald Tribune, *he was present in Dallas when President Kennedy was killed. As an NBC News correspondent, he has covered every national political convention since 1964. He reported for NBC News from Vietnam, Northern Ireland, the Middle East, and, on special assignment, the revolution in Iran. For his reports on the Jordan war, in 1970, he was awarded broadcasting's most coveted prize, the George Foster Peabody Award. He is the author of two novels,* The Southerner *and* Strangers on the Shore, *as well as* Murder on Clam Pond *and* Death at the Cut, *earlier mysteries about Mac McFarland. His articles and short stories have appeared in the* Atlantic Monthly, Harper's, *and the* Yale Review, *among other publications.*